From *The Far Traveller*

"It is very beautiful here," said the Englishman.

"It is, indeed," said Klaus.

"A fine castle."

"We think so," said Klaus with a smile. "No doubt there are many larger and finer, but this is ours." He nodded to the footman, who retired.

"So old," pursued Denmead, "and yet so complete. One feels it ought to have a ghost."

"But it has, *gnä'* Herr. It is said that in times long past there were several, notably a white lady who walked up and down the great stairway, but she has not been seen for very many years. Even my grandfather never saw her. Now there is only the Graf Adhemar."

Denmead's ears seemed to prick up of their own accord.

"Have you ever seen him?"

Klaus laughed indulgently. "We have all seen him, *gnä'* Herr, since he was drowned eighty-six years ago. We of the staff are accustomed to see him; he was much beloved in life and we are—how shall I say it—we are glad he is still with us. Still part of our lives, our young Graf Adhemar Hildebrand. We are proud of him, you understand."

"I begin to understand. And in the village, do they believe in him too?"

"Believe in him? One believes what one sees with one's eyes, *gnä'* Herr. During eighty years very many of the village people have served here; they still do. The Herr may have seen them coming and going, and in the old days when there was much entertaining, many more of them did so. The Herr Graf walks about the castle at night, mein Herr, not every night but very often. If we meet him we stand back respectfully to let him pass as we did when he was in life; sometimes he looks at us and seems pleased and sometimes he smiles. It is all quite natural and pleasant, *gnä'* Herr, when one has known it all one's life."

Books by Manning Coles

Ghost Books
Brief Candles, 1954
Happy Returns (English title: *A Family Matter*), 1955
The Far Traveller (non-series),1956
Come and Go, 1958

The Tommy Hambledon Spy Novels
Drink to Yesterday, 1940
A Toast to Tomorrow (English title: *Pray Silence*), 1940
They Tell No Tales, 1941
Without Lawful Authority, 1943
Green Hazard, 1945
The Fifth Man, 1946
Let the Tiger Die, 1947
With Intent to Deceive (English title: *A Brother for Hugh*), 1947
Among Those Absent, 1948
Diamonds to Amsterdam, 1949
Not Negotiable, 1949
Dangerous by Nature, 1950
Now or Never, 1951
Alias Uncle Hugo (Reprint: *Operation Manhunt*), 1952
Night Train to Paris, 1952
A Knife for the Juggler (Reprint: *The Vengeance Man*), 1953
All that Glitters (English title: *Not for Export*;
Reprint: *The Mystery of the Stolen Plans*), 1954
The Man in the Green Hat, 1955
Basle Express, 1956
Birdwatcher's Quarry (English title: *The Three Beans*), 1956
Death of an Ambassador, 1957
No Entry, 1958
Concrete Crime (English title: *Crime in Concrete*), 1960
Search for a Sultan, 1961
The House at Pluck's Gutter, 1963

Non-Series
This Fortress, 1942
Duty Free, 1959

Short Stories
Nothing to Declare, 1960

Young Adult
Great Caesar's Ghost (English title: *The Emperor's Bracelet*), 1943

The Far Traveller
By Manning Coles

The Rue Morgue Press
Boulder, Colorado

About Manning Coles

MANNING COLES was the pseudonym of two Hampshire neighbors who collaborated on a long series of entertaining spy novels featuring Thomas Elphinstone Hambledon, a modern-language instructor turned British secret agent. Most of Hambledon's exploits were aimed against the Germans and took place from World War I through the Cold War, although his best adventures occurred during World War II, especially when Tommy found himself, for one reason or another, working undercover in Berlin.

Some of those exploits were based on the real-life experiences of the male half of the writing team, Cyril Henry Coles (1899-1965), who lied about his age and enlisted under an assumed name in a Hampshire regiment during World War I while still a teenager. He eventually became the youngest officer in British intelligence, often working behind German lines. After the war, Coles first apprenticed at John I. Thorncroft shipbuilders of Southhampton and then emigrated to Australia where he worked on the railway, as a garage manager, and as a columnist for a Melbourne newspaper before returning to England in 1928.

The following year his future collaborator, Adelaide Frances Oke Manning (1891-1959), rented a flat from Coles' father in East Meon, Hampshire, and the two became neighbors and friends. Educated at the High School for Girls in Turnbridge Wells, Kent, Manning, who was eight years Coles' senior, worked in a munitions factory and later at the War Office during World War I. In 1939 she published a solo novel, *Half-Valdez*, that failed to sell. Shortly after this disappointing introduction to the literary world, Coles and Manning hit upon an idea for a spy novel while having tea and began a collaboration that would last until Manning died in 1958. Coles continued the Hambledon series for an additional three books before he died in 1965.

Critic Anthony Boucher aptly described the Hambledon books as being filled with "good-humored implausibility." That same good humor—and a good deal more implausibility—is to be found in the collaborators' four ghost books, which began with *Brief Candles* in 1954 and included two other books featuring the ghostly Latimers, *Happy Returns* in 1955 (published in England as *A Family Matter*) and *Come and Go* in 1958. The fourth ghost book, *The Far Traveller*, which features a displaced, displeased and deceased German nobleman who finds a movie company employing people of the most common sort invading his castle, appeared in 1956. Appearing in the U.S. under the Coles byline, they were published in England under yet another pseudonym, Francis Gaite. Boucher described this new venture "as felicitously foolish as a collaboration of (P.G.) Wodehouse and Thorne Smith."

For more information on the authors see Tom & Enid's Schantz' introduction to The Rue Morgue Press edition of *Brief Candles*.

The Far Traveller

Chapter 1
SCREEN TESTS

THE CASTLE of Grauhugel stands upon the summit of the gray rocky hill from which it takes its name, one of the Siebengebirge, the Seven Hills by the Rhine, though indeed there are many more than seven and the most famous of them all is Drachenfels. The whole district is closely dotted with small steep hills bearing romantic names such as Devil's Rock, Lion's Castle, The Hermit, the Greater and the Lesser Mount of Olives and even, believe it or not, South View. Many of them have, or had, castles perched upon their tops; most of these are ruinous today, but in the Middle Ages the Siebengebirge must have been a highly desirable residential district closely populated with the nobility and gentry who went out hunting together, married each other's daughters, and quarreled violently over the dowries.

The castle of Grauhugel is not at all ruinous but very well preserved and, like a castle in a fairy story, lifts its pepperbox turrets and machicolated battlements above the tops of the trees which clothe the hill. Grauhugel village lies about the foot of the hill, black-and-white timbered houses shouldering each other crookedly about the tiny square, an ancient inn standing back behind its forecourt, and a still more ancient church knee-deep in close-packed tombstones. The only signs of present-day life are a post office at the grocer's, a petrol pump outside the blacksmith's, and a tattered poster on a barn door advertising a cinema show at Ittenbach, only three miles away.

Very early on a fine June morning, so early that bright dewdrops still glittered upon cobweb and tall grass in the level rays of the rising sun, a group of about twenty people were gathered upon a comparatively level space some halfway up the castle drive. They stood about undecidedly and talked together in low tones, as people do who are waiting indefinitely for something to happen; all but five or six of them were dressed in the costume of the 1860s. The space where they stood was a small green glade running back into the trees; the whole scene had an air of unreality as though set upon a stage.

The six men in modern dress were grouped about a van which was drawn up at the side of the drive; the van doors were open and displayed equipment such as is used in filmmaking. Among other things there was a small dynamo fixed to the floor, and insulated cables led from this to lights upon long swiveling arms. One of the men was assembling a tall rod jointed like a fishing rod; it had a microphone hung from the top end and other wires led from this to the interior of the van. The man finished his task and stood back, holding his rod as though waiting to be told where to cast; his eyes were upon the film director and he looked faintly amused.

"Half an hour before we are due to start," said the director in an angry voice, "he does this. Half an hour!" He was a tall slim young man with a mane of black hair; as he spoke he ran his fingers through it till it stood up like the crest of an agitated cockatoo.

"What happened?"

"He came tittupping down that fantastic stone stairway in the main hall as though he were Titania tripping through the buttercups, the silly blithering idiot—"

"Titania?"

"No. Victor Beauregard, of course. Do you know what his real name is? It's a closely guarded secret, but I do. I was just going to yell to him to watch out, those stairs are worn, when he slipped or turned his ankle or something and came a most almighty purler right down the stairs into the hall. I heard something crack; I hoped it was that damned ornate cigarette case he was blinding us all with last night, but it wasn't. I rushed across to him to help him up, but he yelled at me to leave him alone, he'd broken his leg. He had, too, above the knee."

"Probably painful," said the assistant director, lighting a cigarette. "What did you do?"

"I was so livid I just looked at him and of course everyone rushed round and Aurea screamed. Anyway, the ambulance has just come and now what do I do?" He looked round at the costumed villagers strolling in the glade. "All the extras up and nothing to do with them!" He attacked his hair again.

"Calm yourself, George. We must phone to London for someone else, that's all."

"And who else is there at liberty just now?"

"There's so-and-so—" The assistant director mentioned a well-known name.

"I'm making a romantic musical, not a custard-pie farce! There goes the ambulance. You know, there's a curse or something on this production. When that fellow who was playing the servant let me down at the last moment, I was rather pleased than otherwise, can't stand him, but Victor can act. Looks the part, too, the highborn Graf Adhemar Hildebrand von Grauhugel to the life. Philip, what the hell am I to do? The servant we can replace and there's no such immediate urgency, but the Graf—"

Philip Denmead shook his head and there was a short silence broken by the sound of footsteps as two men came up the drive. They were both young, in their early twenties, the first a fair-haired man of medium height who held himself upright and walked well; he had a pleasant face and a certain air of authority. The other, who walked half a pace behind, was a stocky youth with a round face; he carried a heavy carpetbag in each hand and was plainly a servant. Since they were both dressed in the style of the 1860s George Whatmore took them to be two more of the extras who had been recruited in the village.

"Two more of your people just arrived," he said irritably. "I thought you said they were all here on time."

"They were," said Denmead. "I counted them."

"Then you counted wrong."

"Oh no, I didn't. Besides, I've never seen these two before."

The first of the newcomers came within view of the scene in the glade and his eyebrows went up. He spoke over his shoulder to his servant.

"What is all this gathering, Franz?"

"I could not say, mein Herr."

"The Kermesse, I suppose? I have forgotten the date."

The young man walked on and noticed Whatmore and Denmead looking attentively at him. He in his turn looked them over as though he found their appearance unusual; the tall lanky George Whatmore in wide corduroy trousers and a turtleneck sweater with his hair standing on end, and the short rotund Philip Denmead in a violently patterned sports jacket, a shirt open at the neck, and shabby gray flannel trousers. The newcomers did not hesitate but came straight on; Whatmore, frustrated and irritated, strode up to them and addressed them in German.

"You are late, do you know that?"

The stranger looked bleak for a moment and suddenly smiled.

"Perhaps we are, perhaps we are. What is the date?"

"Date?" repeated Whatmore, staring. "You mean what time is it?"

"No, no. I mean what I said." The young man spoke pleasantly, but the air of authority, which was noticeable in his bearing, was equally plain in his voice.

"The first of June, 1955, since you must put on an act, but you'll find it cuts no ice with me."

"Why not?" said Denmead softly, at his elbow, and Whatmore turned sharply. "I mean," added Denmead, "look at him."

Whatmore did so, just as the newcomer turned to look over the village people. His head went back, his chin came forward, and his eyelids drooped over his eyes; he had more the air of a farmer looking over a herd of valued cattle than of a present-day landowner looking at his tenants. An air of ownership. There was also a resemblance to something or somebody—

"Here," said Whatmore, "who are you?"

The young man's eyebrows lifted a little, but he gave no other sign of having heard the question, and Whatmore tried again.

"Excuse me. May I ask your name?"

"Certainly," said the young man at once. "I am the Graf von Grauhugel."

"The devil you are!"

"Why? You appear to be surprised."

"Surprised. Well, yes. Tell me again who you are, both of you, do you mind?" said Whatmore, again raking up his ill-used hair. "I have had one bad shock already this morning and perhaps I am not quite myself."

"I am sorry to hear that. I am the Graf Adhemar von Grauhugel and this is my servant, Franz. Now, if you will forgive me, I must go on. If you are lodging in the neighborhood, no doubt we shall meet again. *Auf Wiedersehen.*"

He turned to walk on up the hill and the servant followed after; Whatmore, who appeared to be bereft of speech, merely gaped upon them and Denmead shook him by the arm.

"Stop them, stop them! There's your Graf, whoever he is. Walks right, stands right, looks right—damn it, he's the picture on the packet—"

"Stop!" cried Whatmore. "You, mein Herr, Herr Graf, or whatever it is, please!" He ran after them and the Graf stopped. "Excuse me. Can you act?"

"You are a very strange young man," said the Graf, "you ask the oddest questions. Act? When we were children we performed charades at Christmas. Why?"

"It's like this," said Whatmore. "We are making a film, and only this morning my leading man—"

He stopped because the Graf's expression was plainly that of one who had not understood one word of what was said to him.

"I'm sorry," stammered Whatmore, "my German is probably at fault. The film—"

"Your German is very good," said the Graf kindly, "if a little oddly pronounced, but I understand you perfectly well. It is the matter of your speech which puzzles me, not the manner. This film, it comes upon stagnant pools or over the eyes of aging horses—"

"No, no. Not that kind. Cinematograph film. A kind of photography—look here! A joke's all very well, but need you pull my leg quite so hard? If you wanted to prove to me that you can act the Graf von Grauhugel of the 1860s it's all right, you've done it. We've had that. Now I—"

"One moment," said the Graf. "Much of what you say is obscure to me, but I must plead guilty to not having kept abreast of modern inventions. It was negligent of me. Do I gather correctly that you wish me to act in some play or another?"

"That's right," said Whatmore with a gulp. "But—"

"And there is some connection with photography?"

"That's right. We photograph the play and then many people can see it. You know all about it, of course you do. Everyone knows about films."

The servant Franz spoke for the first time and then only two words.

"Lantern slides," he said.

"Ah," said the Graf. "Of course. A picture transparency with a light behind and you see it in the dark on a white screen. Correct?"

"Well, we're getting on," said Whatmore in a resigned tone. "There's rather more to it than that in these days, but that's the general idea." He paused and brushed his hands over his eyes. "I can't imagine why you want to play a game like this when I've told you I'm convinced already, but have it your own way. My leading man fell downstairs this morning and broke his leg so I am looking for someone to take his place. Is that clear?"

"Perfectly. Most unfortunate. And it is his part which you wish me to undertake?"

Whatmore, convinced that these two men were behaving like this for the express purpose of being chosen to play the two leads, was seized with an access of caution.

"Well, if the screen tests are satisfactory—"

"And what is the play?" asked the Graf. "One of our heroic German epics or something lighter, more in the French vein?"

Whatmore blinked. "Well, neither. It is what I should call a romantic musical—"

"I was always musical," said the Graf, nodding his head. "A light opera, like *Martha?*"

"Not so much music as that. Spoken dialogue and normal acting, but with a number of songs here and there. More of the type of *White Horse Inn* or *The Student Prince.*"

"I believe it will make a very pleasant entertainment," said the Graf. "May I ask if you have yet selected the subject? Or are you performing some play already written?"

"Of course it's been written and scripted and all; we were ready to begin producing when that bumble-footed nincompoop fell down the stairs. It's a local story, that's why we are filming it here, or most of it. It's based on the life of that Graf von Grauhugel who was drowned in 1869— What's the matter?"

For the Graf Adhemar had taken two paces back and seemed to be leaning against his servant for support. Upon his face there came that moonlike expression which may be seen when a man has been told some unexpected piece of news which at once stuns and delights him; such as that he holds the winning ticket in the Irish Sweep. The Graf's face crimsoned and his eyes twinkled, but his mouth was as firm and straight as ever; his servant's imperturbable face was still wooden, but the round blue eyes rounded a little more.

"It is nothing," said the Graf, recovering himself. "A momentary dizziness, no more. Yes, I should think you could weave a pleasant comedy out of his story. I do not mind spending an afternoon or two impersonating your hero."

"An afternoon or two! A month's hard work," said Whatmore. "It's a job, you understand, and I am prepared to pay you for it; if the screen tests are satisfactory, that is."

"I could not possibly consider—"

"I'm afraid I can't wait," said Whatmore, and made him an offer in marks per day.

The Graf stared at him coldly and the director hastily added half as much again, the Graf blinked but did not answer, and Whatmore doubled his original offer.

"And that's my final word," he added. "Hang it, I'm not J. Arthur Rank."

The Graf moved suddenly as though he had been energetically nudged from behind, and nodded his head.

"Well, that's settled if the screen tests are OK. Philip! I am giving this gentleman a screen test, get cracking, will you? By the way, my name is Whatmore and this is my assistant director, Philip Denmead. Philip, this is—what is your real name?"

"Von Grauhugel," said the Graf, with a polite bow for each of them.

"That really is your name, is it? One of the same family, eh? It'll look rather funny on the cast list, don't you th—"

"And this is my servant, Franz Bagel. He also takes his part, please. That is a *sine qua non*."

"Oh, is it? Well, we'll see. Oh, Philip, pay off those extras and send them home. We'll let them know later tonight whether we shall want them tomorrow. Now, Herr von Grauhugel—"

" 'Herr Graf' would be correct, please."

"Sorry. Herr Graf it shall be. Now, if you don't mind waiting a moment while we get the cameras lined up. Bert, long and medium shots first, I'll bring in close-ups later."

The Herr Graf beguiled the time of waiting by strolling across to stand near the small table at which Denmead sat to pay off the extras. Names were called out which appeared to interest the Graf and his servant alike; when the name of Bagel was called and a very pretty girl came up for her ten marks, Franz watched her every movement and the Graf grinned at him over his shoulder. The villagers glanced shyly at the two men but said nothing; one old woman near the end of the line looked intently at the Graf and dropped a curtsey. The Graf nodded casually and Whatmore, watching closely, said: "He'll do," under his breath.

Then the tests began. The camera produced a whirring noise and the Graf stopped suddenly to look at it.

"Don't look at the camera unless I tell you to do so," said Whatmore. "Look anywhere else, but never straight at the camera."

"I only wondered where the noise came from. Is that the camera? Indeed! Am I being photographed now? I thought I was doing this just to show you, no?" He smiled deprecatingly at Whatmore and the faithful camera recorded every smallest change in expression. "You must tell me if I am doing right; I am a child in these matters, you must remember."

Whatmore strolled forward. "I am a stranger; you have just seen me. Walk up to me and ask me who I am and what I want. You are the owner, of course."

"Do I like the look of you, or not?"

"Not much."

The Graf obeyed and Whatmore nodded. "Thank you. Now with your servant. Stand there, please, facing this way. Franz, come up from behind him and tell him a piece of good news. Herr Graf, you turn when you hear him coming."

Franz walked up with his usual wooden expression and said: "May it please the Herr Graf—"

The Graf hardly moved. "Well?" he said, tossing the word over his shoulder.

"Ah," said Whatmore to himself.

"Your highborn Aunt Eugenie has been struck by lightning," said Franz.

The Graf turned and burst into a peal of laughter in which Franz joined by allowing his face to split momentarily into a wide grin which immediately vanished again, leaving no trace behind.

"Thank you," said Whatmore. "Now—"

A few more tests followed and eventually the Graf said: "You know, Herr Whatmore, I had no idea that acting was like this. It isn't really, is it? I thought one made studied gestures"—he threw his arms out—"or tore one's hair. You were acting when we first came up, were you not?"

Whatmore nearly blushed. "It all depends what character you are portraying."

"And you just want me to behave naturally?"

"Just that."

"How very unexpected," said the Graf.

"Now for Franz. You can go off the set, Herr Graf."

"Off the—?"

"Come over here. Franz, you see that big tree over there, a little by itself?"

"Yes, mein Herr."

"Start over here by the edge of the drive. You are strolling quietly along by yourself when you suddenly notice that there is a pretty girl hiding behind the tree."

"Mein Herr?"

"Well?"

"It would be easier if there really was one."

"Franz," said the Graf.

"Very good, Herr Graf," said Franz. He went off to the edge of the drive and turned.

"Mein Herr?"

"Well?"

"Am I in the presence of the Herr Graf? In the play, that is?"

"No. You are out by yourself."

Franz strolled along and even his face was different because the wooden control had been taken off. He picked up a thin switch and made it sing through the air, he paused to listen to the note of a bird. He looked at ease, relaxed, more natural, and much more impudent. His eye fell upon the lonely tree and he checked momentarily, then he looked away and wandered vaguely in its direction. When he was some fifteen yards from the tree he made a sudden dash for it and with a whoop of joy, swung round it and disappeared from sight.

Whatmore waited to see him reappear round the bole, but he did not; the director signed to the cameraman and walked forward.

"Where's the fellow gone?"

"I am here, mein Herr," said Franz, and stepped out from a covert further back.

"How the hell did you manage that?"

"But it is what one would do," protested Franz, "if one saw a pretty girl."

"What?"

"Disappear into the wood, mein Herr."

"That will do, Franz," said the Graf.

Chapter 2
CURTAINS

"TAKE THAT FILM UP to Jones at once, please, Bert," said Whatmore, addressing the cameraman. "Tell him I shall want to see the rushes this evening. Denmead, we shall want voice tests. Do you think we could borrow some curtains and drape a room with them? See the majordomo, will you? If we can get a room fixed up we could do the tests this afternoon. Oh, by the way, Herr Graf, can you speak English?"

"I can a very little speak," said the Graf, "and still better I onnerstan'. My servant, too. But like the native, no."

"That won't matter as your speeches are written out for you, so the wording will be all right. Since you are a German in the film, a foreign accent will be an asset. Like the late much lamented Conrad Veidt's. Victor Beauregard was not too good at that. See to it, Philip, will you?"

"I will," said Denmead.

"Do you wish my presence any longer now?" asked the Graf.

"Not at the moment, thank you. This afternoon we will test your voice and this evening you shall see for yourself how you act"

"Thank you so much," said the Graf. He nodded kindly to Whatmore and Denmead, threw one more wondering glance at the van and its appurtenances, and walked on toward the castle, closely followed by Franz, again loaded down with the carpetbags.

"I don't get it at all," said Whatmore, watching them. "He's putting on an act, of course, to show me he can do it. Quite a good idea, but why keep it up?"

"Well, he hadn't got the job yet," said Denmead.

"He has, but he doesn't know it. I mean, we must see the rushes of course, but there's no doubt in my mind. I wonder who he really is."

"Can't he be the, or a, Graf von Grauhugel?"

"No, that's the one person I'm quite sure he can't be. Graf is a title, like duke, and there's never more than one at a time. You can't imagine two simultaneous dukes of Norfolk, can you? Well, I know the present Graf von Grauhugel very well, a tall dark fellow with a scar down one cheek which he got at Arnhem. I took him prisoner later and we got on rather well. I used to go and see him. He came and stayed with me after the war."

"He's not here, is he? What happens if he comes home?"

"He won't. He's stuck in London for six months, taking an intensive course in metallurgy, I think it is. I told him about my father and the 'one more chance' before I throw all this up and go into the business—I must make a success of this, Philip."

"Why? What is the business?"

"Enameled iron utensils," said Whatmore curtly.

"Oh."

"My father has a chain of cinemas, too. I think he bought them as a hobby, or something, so if this film is any good I shall at least get a showing. He's rather interested in cinematography, but he's a pretty severe critic. I mean, the film will have to be good; the mere fact that I made it won't affect his judgment."

"I see," said Denmead.

"I told the Graf—my Graf, his name's Sigmund—about it and that I wanted to make a musical, but I hadn't even got a story and not much money. So he told me about this Graf Adhemar, who was quite a lad in his day, and we worked up a story between us. He told me about this castle, too, and showed me some photographs. He said I could borrow the castle while he's away, it would do the place good to be lived in, keep the servants on their toes and all that. He keeps a skeleton staff here and it doesn't cost me anything."

"Did you save his life?" asked Denmead. "I mean, all this is pretty wholesale—"

"Oh, rot," said George Whatmore. "He's a good scout, the Graf Sigmund, and he's not using his castle at the moment. In fact, I don't think he has lived here since his father died about four years ago. But that's how I know for a fact that this one is phony. If he persists much longer I shall tell him about Sigmund and see how he laughs that one off."

"I suppose he's some German actor—"

"He's an actor all right."

"Probably blotted his copybook somehow and wants to work his passage back. I tell you what," said Denmead, "if you do put him on the payroll he'll have to give us his right name."

"So he will. Of course he will; as soon as he's landed the job all this nonsense will stop. Here's Aurea, we must tell her about him."

Aurea Goldie came down the drive to meet them, a golden girl who matched her name. In strict accuracy, the name had been well chosen to match the girl, but no reasonable person would expect a film actress to struggle on under the handicap of Doris Hodgkinson. She had hair which was naturally the exact color of a gold sovereign, if anyone in these days remembers what color they were; a golden skin just flushed with rose, darker eyebrows and eyelashes, and very blue eyes. She was still very young, which accounted for Whatmore's having been able to afford her; in a couple of years' time, if all went well, she would be far out of his financial reach. In the meantime she was a sensible lighthearted young woman and thrilled to the spine with living in a real, genuinely medieval castle.

"Poor Victor," she said, rather perfunctorily, "isn't it too frightful? Have you rung up about him?"

"No, my child," said Whatmore, who was almost ten years her senior, "I have not. He is but even now arriving at the hospital and being lifted tenderly from the ambulance by squads of assiduous houris. Is he not, Victor Beauregard? And don't try to put that mournful look over on me, you hated him really, didn't you?"

She laughed. "Not so bad as that, I only hated being patronized. If he'd called me 'dear little lady' just twice more, something too frightful would have happened. I say, who is the marvelous young man who's just

arrived at the castle? The servants are running round him like tame rab-
bits and practically bending double whenever he deigns to look at them.
The company all assumed that he was your friend the Graf Sigmund."

"Oh, did they?" said Whatmore slowly. "No, that isn't Sigmund, that's
Victor Beauregard's stand-in, the new Graf Adhemar von Grauhugel.
Think you'll be able to play opposite to him, Aurea?"

"Oh, indeed? I am surprised. Is that who he is? Yes. Yes, I should
think some of those scenes should go over big."

"Fine," said Whatmore. "Splendid, in fact. By the way, I must go and
see about his being billeted in the castle, there are plenty of spare rooms,
it's only to—"

"That's all right," said Aurea. "That's all sewn up, tacked down, and
ironed flat. That's why everybody thought he was the Graf Sigmund."

"What—"

"I was standing at the back of the hall there, airing my best German
on that cherubic old pet, the majordomo, when this man—what's his
name?"

"I haven't quite got it," said Whatmore. "I must ask him again. Go
on."

"Let's call him X. He walked in, stopped just inside the door, and
looked about him as though he'd bought the place. The majordomo stopped
in the middle of a word and substituted a gasp for the end of it. I looked at
him and he'd turned a most peculiar color. He forgot about me and tottered forward. X looked him up and down and said: 'What's your name?'
My elderly friend bowed till his nose bumped his knees and said: 'Klaus
Förster, Highborn.' X nodded as though it wasn't of much importance
and looked round the hall again. Then he stared at the blank space over
the fireplace and said 'Where's the picture?' Poor old Klaus asked what
picture, and X said: 'Judith and Holofernes, of course. Someone has moved
it. Why?' Klaus said he did not know why, Highborn, but it was now in
the banqueting hall, Highborn. Then X started off for the stairs and Klaus
just hopped out of his way in time. When he—X—had gone up two or
three steps he suddenly saw me, stopped dead, and bowed as though I was
royalty, so I dropped him my best curtsey I learned in *Rosenkavalier* and
walked slowly away."

"Didn't he follow you?" asked Whatmore.

"No, he went straight on up the stairs. I heard—"

"Provoking," murmured Whatmore.

"Be quiet," said Aurea. "I heard later that that suite of rooms off the
picture gallery—"

"Picture gallery," said Whatmore. "Got it."

"Got what?"

"Where I'd seen that face before. Never mind. What about the rooms? Which ones?"

"That shut-up suite all under dust sheets they showed us yesterday, with the painted ceilings. The haunted rooms, they called them. Lily says there are simply scores of housemaids scurrying in and out, taking things in and carrying things away. I think Lily exaggerates; there wouldn't be more than a dozen housemaids even in a castle like this, would there?"

"Don't ask me. Who's Lily, for heaven's sake?"

"My maid. You've seen her scores of times."

"Lily, for some reason," said Whatmore, "never makes even the most temporary dent in my stream of consciousness. Can one dent a stream? Never mind. So long as she's not another member of my cast whom I've never seen before and know nothing about, pass, Lily, all's well."

"Look here, George, what is all this? Who is this man and where did you find him?"

"I didn't, he found me. I was just tearing my hair because we'd got the whole place botching with extras all dressed up and no leading man and no servant, when this fellow strolls up and engages us in conversation. No, I spoke to him, it doesn't matter. He was dressed like the others and I took them to be some of the extras—he had his man with him. Then Philip Denmead pointed out— By the way, where is Philip? He was here just now."

"I don't know," said Aurea, looking vaguely about her, "he must have drifted off. What did he point out?"

"That these two were obviously the ideal Graf-and-servant pair. He was quite right, too, they are. So we gave both of them screen tests and you shall see the rushes tonight."

"But what's his name?"

"Well, that's where I fall down," said Whatmore. "I asked his name and he said he was the Graf Adhemar von Grauhugel and this was his servant, Franz. At least, I took it that he meant that was his name, but I see now he only meant that that was what they would be in the film, if you get me. So I said all right, tell me your real names presently or something like that and then forgot to ask him again. I'll get them later on, there's no immediate hurry. We're doing the voice tests this afternoon and, by the way, I expect that's where Philip has gone. To fix the room up. I told him to ask the majordomo for some curtains."

"I think he'll find the majordomo is busy," said Aurea thoughtfully.

"Look here, why did he practically kiss the ground in front of X if he wasn't absolutely Somebody? I mean, you should have seen it, and all the other servants too."

"I am coming to think that X is a member of the family. I think we want capitals there, The Family. He is the living image of one of the pictures in the gallery, though I couldn't remember till you mentioned it where I'd seen that face before. Odd things, family likenesses. They crop up. Oh, and of course that accounts for his knowing about the film; I expect Sigmund wrote and told him."

"Quite simple," said Aurea, "when you know how it's done. Well, shall we walk up?"

After a long and baffling pursuit, Denmead succeeded in literally cornering the majordomo at a turn in one of the twisting passages.

"Look here. Stop a moment, please. I want to speak to you."

Denmead had learned his German as a prisoner of war in Germany; it was fluent and reasonably accurate but had its limitations. When he thought that he had captured the majordomo's wandering attention, he went on.

"I do not wish to give you more trouble than I can avoid, but might I borrow some curtains?"

"Curtains," said the old man vaguely.

"Curtains. It does not matter how old and ragged they are, what color they are, or even what they are made of. Just curtains."

"In order to produce the right kind and size," said old Klaus, "may I know for what purpose the Herr requires them?"

"I want to hang them round the walls of a room."

For the first time Denmead was assured that the majordomo really awoke to his presence and the meaning of what he said. Klaus was a handsome old man, though in build he was short and broad; he had a head like one of the more reputable Roman emperors on a coin, black hair gone iron gray but still thick, a brown skin, black eyebrows and eyelashes, and oddly light gray eyes. The eyes turned upon Denmead and lit up with surprise and what might have been amusement.

"The gracious Herr requires a room with curtains hung all round the walls—so?"

"Exactly so. Do you happen to have one? I don't know whether you would understand, but I want to take a voice test, and for that—"

But the old man did not wait to hear the explanation. He said: "Be pleased, if you will, to follow me," and turned to lead the way back along the passage by which he had come; even as he turned his head away Denmead would have sworn that he saw a smile curl up the corners of the old man's mouth.

They went along the passage, down a narrow and steep stair, and came out in a corridor along which Denmead faintly remembered having been conducted in the course of yesterday's tour of the castle. The major-domo stopped.

"Those large doors beyond are those of the castle chapel, which I showed to you yesterday, but we go in here."

He unhooked a large bunch of keys which hung from his belt, selected one of them, and opened the door of a room next the chapel; the door was noticeably wide but was not otherwise remarkable. When they went inside, the room proved to be of a fair size, totally empty except for a small table against the wall at the far end, and decorated only by very dark curtains which covered the walls from the ceiling to the floor, all round except for one window over the table. Denmead looked about him and nodded appreciatively.

"The curtains," said Klaus, "can be drawn over the window also if required."

"I don't think we need bother with that. I think that this will do perfectly well if we may use it. It will only be for a short time. Is there any electricity in here?"

"No. This room is but very seldom used and when it is we bring in candles."

"It does not matter; my electrician can run a wire in from the nearest power point. Thank you very much. We will come in this afternoon, then." Denmead walked out and turned in the doorway. "Rather a gloomy room, is it not? I am not surprised you don't use it much."

Klaus again looked faintly amused but said no more. Denmead returned to the entrance hall and met Aurea Goldie and Whatmore coming in.

"There is a room here which is fully draped already," he said. "I think it will do perfectly; come and look at it. There's only one thing; no electricity in there. Is Harry about? I want him to take a lead in."

"You carry on," said Whatmore. "If you say it's all right, that goes; I'll see it later."

The Graf lunched in his suite alone, with Franz to wait on him.

"This is very pleasant, Franz," he said. "It is like the old days come back—almost."

"There are changes," said Franz. "One must, naturally, expect it, but this is a strange world we have come back to. When I went down for the Herr's hot water I was told that there was no need to carry it up, it was 'hot in the tap.' I did not wish to arouse surprise by asking, but, mein Herr, what is this 'hot in the tap'?"

"There is a place through here," said the Graf, abandoning his stewed veal for the moment. "Come and look. When Klaus showed me in here he opened this door and called the room a 'bathroom.' Look, there are many taps; we have met taps before, if you remember, in England when we were there. They only gave one cold water, you remember, but no doubt some of these run hot." He turned on one which was labeled W, for "warm," stuck his finger under it and pulled it out hastily. "Ach! A wonder indeed. It all but boils. Very well arranged."

"And what a huge bath," said Franz, wide-eyed. "The Herr Graf can step into that and lie down at full length. But what to do with the water after? That must be taken away."

"There is a hole," said the Graf, poking it with his finger. "I assume it falls down there and one of the scullions catches it at the bottom. There will be one whose business it is to wait for it to fall down."

"Excellent," said Franz. "I always thought it would be less trouble to pour it out of the window. But, Herr Graf, your meat is cooling."

Presently Franz asked if his Herr had decided to consent to act in this new kind of play.

"Yes, of course," said the Graf. "Why not? Indeed, I have no choice, since this is my chance to do what should have been done eighty-six years ago. I am anxious, Franz, to finish it now and go home; it wearies me to linger here, and all this time the Gräfin waits. If it were not for you, Franz, I would have despaired long ago. I never forget, not for a single moment, that there was no need for you to be here but that you chose to stay with me." He looked at Franz with great affection.

"When we were very little boys," said Franz, "we played together. When we were older I became your servant, it was said. In fact, I was always your servant and always shall be, what should I do alone? Time goes on and so do we."

There was a short pause.

"Besides, mein Herr, it was all your fault," said Franz in a lighter tone. "You should have learned to swim."

"Nonsense. It would not have helped at all. You could swim, but you were drowned all the same. About this acting. The one thing which jars upon me is this business of being paid for it. I was never paid for anything in all my life, I paid other people. It is not dignified."

"But it will be very useful," urged Franz. "Look now, mein Herr, you had brothers and doubtless they had children. There is no doubt a present-day Graf von Grauhugel though he does not seem to be here. He, of course, draws the revenue from the estates while we are penniless."

His master laughed. "That is quite true, but do we need money? They will feed us here and what more do we need?"

"Much more. We need clothes such as other men wear; these we have are out of date and if we go out we shall be stared at. Laughed at, especially by the girls. 'Why,' they will say, 'do you go about in granddad's trousers?' Terrible, mein Herr."

"You are right. When I am paid, we will go shopping in Cologne."

"There is another matter which had crossed my mind," said Franz, a little apologetically. "The name. Could the name of the Graf Adhemar Hildebrand von Grauhugel appear on a payroll?"

"No. Certainly not. That settles the question of pay; I cannot take it. Pour me a glass of wine, Franz, I have eaten enough."

"When we were twenty," said Franz, doing as he was bid, "we went to Paris."

"Ah," said the Graf, and a reminiscent gleam came into his eyes.

"While we were there, the gracious Herr did not always call himself von Grauhugel. Eh?"

"That is true. It would not always have been convenient. What did I call myself, Franz? Herr—something—"

"Reisenfern. Johann Reisenfern, a good name, it sounds well. So true, also, the far traveller."

"Still true. So you wish me to become again the modest Johann Reisenfern? I suppose, if you have made up your mind to it, I must agree."

"In order that we may buy ourselves new trousers," agreed Franz. "Beautiful large corduroy ones, like the Herr Whatmore's."

There came a knock at the door. Franz answered it and came back with a message.

"The Herr Whatmore's compliments and all is now ready for the voice test."

"We come," said the Graf, tossing off his wine and springing to his feet. "Shall I have to sing, Franz, do you think? It is long since I felt like singing, but I could today. 'La Donna è Mobile,' " he warbled in a pleasing tenor voice. "There should be a guitar accompaniment; I wonder whether mine is still about."

They found Whatmore waiting at the foot of the great flying staircase which came down into the middle of the entrance hall.

"Where will you hear me," asked the Graf, "here?"

"Well, no. We have a room fixed up for it; will you come with me? You see, to get the true tones of a voice without echo or resonance," said Whatmore, leading the way with long strides, "it is necessary to hang curtains along the walls. Denmead, my assistant, asked the majordomo and he was most helpful. It's along here, somewhere. Denmead! Where are you?"

"Here," said Denmead, stepping out of a doorway. "Mind the cables lying along the floor. In here."

"Good gracious," said Whatmore, looking round at the black hangings. "Do you know what this is?"

"No idea," said Denmead cheerfully. "It's got curtains all round, that's all I'm interested in. Why?"

"It's the mortuary chamber, that's why," said Whatmore, and turned to apologize to the Graf only to find that he was struggling with suppressed laughter and his servant's face was wearing a wide grin. "Why, have you been in here before?"

"Oh yes," said the Graf. "Once. But it was a long time ago."

Chapter 3
JOHANN REISENFERN

AFTER DINNER that evening there came another messenger to knock at the door of the Graf's suite. "The Herr Whatmore's compliments and the cinema films are ready to be seen."

"The Herr Graf shall be informed," said Franz, and shut the door again. "The lantern slides await your presence, mein Herr."

"He did not say 'lantern slides,' did he? He used that word with which the Herr Whatmore puzzled me this morning. Film. The something film. Let us go, we shall soon find out."

They were led to a room furnished principally with half a dozen rows of assorted chairs and a large boxlike object upon a stand at the back. The chairs faced a blank wall with a white screen upon it. Most of the film company were present; also a few of the servants, who got up when the Graf entered and stood deferentially against the walls, nor could they be persuaded to sit down again though there were seats to spare.

"Thank you," said the majordomo in a hushed voice such as is customary in churches, "thank you, but we stand. We are not in the way, here?"

"Not at all, but surely you must be glad to sit down," said Denmead kindly. "You have been on your feet all day."

"The gracious Herr is most thoughtful," said old Klaus, "but, asking pardon, we will not sit. It would not be fitting."

"But," said Denmead, "you have always sat down at these shows before—"

"Before," said Klaus firmly, "was different."

Aurea Goldie came in with Whatmore. The Graf, who had seated himself without hesitation in the middle chair of the front row, sprang to his feet to be presented.

"Aurea, this is the new Graf von Grauhugel, your opposite number. Herr Graf, this is the Fräulein Aurea Goldie, who plays the part of your jilted fiancée."

The Graf bowed with deep respect and kissed her hand; Aurea, once more recalling *Der Rosenkavalier,* dropped a most excellent curtsey.

"And am I supposed," asked the Graf, "even in a play, to be so lost to all sense of beauty, decorum, and common sense as to jilt one so charming and so lovely? Impossible!"

Aurea curtseyed again, the moment seemed to demand it.

"I'm afraid so," said Whatmore. "Now, if you'll all sit down we'll put the lights out and get on with the show. Please sit down. Why are those people standing at the back there? There are plenty of chairs."

"Let them alone," said Denmead, "they'd rather stand. To sit," he added in a low voice, "it would not be fitting." He glanced pointedly at the back of the Graf's shining blond head bent toward Aurea's in an attitude of deferential attention. The servant, Franz Bagel, was standing against the wall at the end of the row; even as Whatmore looked at them the Graf turned his head and his eyes met his servant's for a passing moment before the lights went out.

A square of light appeared on the screen, remained for a few moments, and was then replaced by a scene in a woodland glade. There was one figure in the foreground, a young man with his back turned to the camera. Suddenly he whirled round and the inquiring eyes looked straight at the audience . . . .

The Graf sprang to his feet with a yelp of surprise and cast a large shadow upon the picture. Whatmore said: "Sit down, please," in an authoritative voice and Aurea Goldie reached up to lay a hand on the Graf's arm. He collapsed into his seat again and already Franz was beside him, crouched on the floor at his knee.

"But that is I, myself," muttered the Graf. "Even as I looked and moved—"

"It is nothing," murmured Franz. "It is but an improvement upon the pictures which we were shown in Paris. In these days, now, they appear to move, that is all."

"I remember now," said the Graf. "There was also an arrangement of a round thing with mirrors which made figures appear to dance. A zoetrope, it was called."

The low rapid German baffled Aurea Goldie, who understood none of it.

"You have not seen yourself on a film before?" she said. "It is a startling experience at first."

"It startled me, *gnädiges* Fräulein," admitted the Graf. "It is like our legend of the *Doppelgänger,* a most unlucky thing to see."

"I hope that this one will be very lucky for you. Look, now you are speaking to George Whatmore."

The little scenes unrolled one after the other. The Graf, with an imperious gesture, pointed out the way down the drive to George Whatmore, who walked resignedly away; Franz told his master something which amused him— "Franz—oh, he's gone. Franz is very good, is he not? So natural. I should know him anywhere."

"You are both good," said Aurea. "Where did you get your training?"

"I beg your pardon?"

"Your experience. You must have done quite a lot of this sort of part, your carriage and gestures are so right."

"Thank you very much," murmured the Graf.

"All those little differences of look and manner between men of that date and men of today. It's not easy to define, but you have it. Victor Beauregard is a good actor, but he was too modern, somehow. Do you know what I mean?"

"Victor Beauregard. He was the man who fell down the stair, was he not? Did you like him, *gnä'* Fräulein?"

Aurea was swept away by a sudden rush of truth to the tongue.

"I couldn't stand him at any price!"

"That is well. He was not good for you."

"How do you know? You were not here—"

The strip of film ran out, the lights were turned on again, and Whatmore came to speak to them.

"Well? What did you think of that?"

"A most interesting experience," said the Graf smoothly.

"Very good indeed," said Aurea.

"I agree," said Whatmore. "Well, you've landed the part."

"I beg your pardon?"

"I said, you've landed the part. You will be the Graf Adhemar von Grauhugel in this film and your servant will be your servant. There are, of course, a number of small points which will want to be put right, but we can deal with them as we come to them. I'll give you a copy of the script for you to study. Denmead! Have you got two copies of the script there? One for—by the way, now you're engaged, what is your name?"

The Graf hesitated. "Er—Johann Reisenfern."

"Reisenfern. Reis—how do you spell it? Reisenfern, I see. Is that your real name?"

"No," said the Graf coldly. "Why?"

"Sorry," said Whatmore. "No business of mine. And your servant?"

"Franz Bagel."

"But that is his name in the film."

"It may well be so," said the Graf patiently. "Bagel is a name commonly found in this district and Franz was the name given him by his parents. I believe you have another Bagel among the villagers who were assembled here this morning. Annchen. Rather pretty."

"That's right," said Philip Denmead. "This village seems to be largely populated with Bagels."

"A prolific family," said the Graf, without a smile.

"Very. Well, here's your script and here's another for Franz, where is — oh, there you are. Take care of them, I haven't got enough copies as it is."

"Have we," said the Graf, looking through the wad of typewritten pages, "to learn all these speeches by heart?"

"Not all at once. One scene at a time will do. Then, as we get each scene in the can, you may forget it and go on to the next. It's not like a stage play where you have to repeat the whole thing at each performance, but of course you know all about that. You ought to find this simple in comparison," said Whatmore.

"In comparison—"

"With what you're used to, for there's no doubt you are an actor. That was why I asked if Reisenfern was your real name; I expected it to be one which I had heard before."

A slow grin spread across the Graf's expressive face.

"As a matter of fact," he admitted, "it is."

"I am not asking," said Whatmore hastily. "No doubt you have your reasons."

"Thank you so much," said the Graf. "Most kind." He bowed to Aurea Goldie, nodded kindly to the rest of the company, and strolled grace-
fully out of the room with Franz, carrying both scripts, at his heels.

"Well!" said Whatmore, looking after them. "Did you get anything
out of him, m'dear?"

"Nothing," said Aurea. "I asked him where he had gained his previ-
ous experience and he sidestepped it. I tell you one thing, he has never
acted in films before. We all know what a shock it is the first time one
sees oneself on a film, but he was startled into fits. One would almost
think—"

"What?"

"Nothing," said Aurea.

"One would almost think," prompted Denmead, "that he'd never seen
a moving picture before."

"But that's absurd," said Whatmore.

"That's why I didn't say it," said Aurea.

"When Franz dived across to him," said Denmead, "didn't you hear
what they said?"

"My German is not so terribly good," she said. "They talked so fast
and so low that I only caught one word."

"And that was—"

"Mirrors."

"Mirrors? What, 'it's all done with mirrors'? Oh, surely not," said
Whatmore.

"Spiegel is mirror, isn't it?"

"You must have been mistaken," said Whatmore.

"Have it your own way," said Aurea. "I daresay you're right. Oh, by
the way, one thing did emerge. He knows Victor Beauregard."

"Oh, does he? What did he say?"

"Very little, it was just at the last moment before the lights came on
again. He merely remarked quite casually that Victor was not a very nice
person, or words to that effect."

"Oh, really. Interesting. Well, perhaps Victor, when he rises from his
bed of pain, will be able to tell us who Reisenfern really is," said Whatmore.

"But—" said Aurea.

"But what?"

"Why do you want to know?"

"Just idle curiosity," said Whatmore.

"But if he wants to keep it quiet—"

"You don't seriously suppose," put in Denmead, "that any of us here will ever see Beauregard again unless we encounter him casually some time in the unforeseeable future, do you? As soon as his leg is set he will be tenderly conveyed to the airport and there carried upon a stretcher into an airliner leaving for London. That's Beauregard, that was. We've had him."

"Suits me," said Aurea. "Well, I'm going up, I've got to prompt Lily about a dress. Good night, everybody."

"I didn't know she disliked Beauregard as much as that," said Whatmore, "did you?"

"She's too good a trouper to have said so earlier," said Denmead, "but it was pretty obvious. 'Victor,' " he quoted, "'was not a very nice person.

"Providence," said Whatmore thoughtfully, "pushed him down the stairs."

On the first floor, in the pleasant suite which was said to be haunted, the Graf was so deeply immersed in the script that time flowed by unnoticed. Eventually Franz, who had been hovering uneasily for some minutes, ventured to interrupt.

"By permission, Herr Graf—"

"Franz," said the Graf, looking up, "this is funny. It's absurd, it's fantastic, it's comic. Who wrote this stuff, the Graf Sigmund?"

"I could not say, Herr Graf. Excuse me—"

"The things I am supposed to have said! Baa, baa! Franz, am I a sheep?"

"Definitely not, mein Herr. But, by permission—"

"Listen. This is me talking. 'My mother, ma'am, has encouraged me to hope that I may dare to offer you my addresses.' Franz, is that any way to ask a girl to marry you?"

"It is not a method I should myself employ. But—"

"And what does she say? Does she say, 'If you need so much encouragement—' "

Franz picked up a silver spoon and struck twelve ringing notes upon a glass on the table.

"What are you playing at?"

"By permission, twelve o'clock striking. In two minutes Old Jakob"— the castle clock—"will say the same. It is time, mein Herr, for you to haunt the castle."

"What, now? What, still? But I am here in residence, Franz, surely that will do. Have I really got to wander about these long passages and finally ooze through that silly door which was walled up in 1890 to stop me doing it—"

"Yes, mein Herr, if it please you—"

"Or even if it doesn't, I suppose," grumbled the Graf, heaving himself out of his comfortable chair. "Just a moment while I immaterialize—"

"Oh, be quick! The clock—"

Old Jakob in the main tower chimed for the hour and then struck midnight on a deep-toned bell. Inside the castle all was quiet; since the film company were about early in the mornings they did not usually stay up late at night. The figure of the Graf, not solid nor yet transparent but as though made of low gray light, moved soundlessly about. George Whatmore, returning, sponge in hand, from the bathroom to his bedroom, caught an uncertain glimpse of it as it turned a corner and was lost to sight. Whatmore hung on his heel for a moment and then entered his bedroom and shut the door behind him.

"I must be tired," he said to himself. "Eyestrain." He got into bed, switched out the light, and was immediately asleep.

Downstairs, the dimly lit passages were deserted and the spacious rooms empty and silent; but in the great hall, by the service door in the shadow of the stairway, there stood a group of six or eight people close together and, a little in front of them, the square figure of Klaus Förster, the majordomo.

"He is not coming," said a voice from the back of the group.

"Silence," said Klaus.

Presently the slim gray figure of the Graf Adhemar crossed the hall toward the foot of the stairway; as he came he took something from an immaterial pocket and began to toss it in the air and catch it again as he walked.

"He is pleased," murmured one of the group. "He does that when he is pleased."

"He is smiling," whispered another. "Look, he is smiling."

The gray figure passed unhurriedly up the stairway and out of sight.

"A-ah," said the company, who appeared to have been holding their breath.

"There," said Klaus, "you see? What did I tell you? He is here as he always was. It is ridiculous and impertinent to suggest that the gracious Herr who came today is he. It is true that the likeness is great—"

"Klaus Förster," said the head cellarer, "do not lecture us, please. We are not underservants beginning our training. As for thinking that the gracious Herr just arrived is our Graf in human form, you were the first to think so. I was passing through the hall when he came in and I saw your face, also your knees knocking together. Also, you called him by the Graf's own title, *Hochwohlgeboren.* Also—"

"I was startled," admitted Klaus. "In part, because of the dress, which is in every respect the same. But now I have seen our own Graf again, there are differences. Our visitor is a little taller, I think, and a little stouter in build, also he moves more decisively. No, he is—"

"But who is he, Klaus?" asked another. "He is one of the highborn family, the likeness is so great. Yes, yes, I saw you go to look at the picture in the long gallery. I had been looking at it myself."

"I do not know who he is," admitted Klaus, "and I should know them all after all these years. But there are many cousins, as you know. He wishes to be known as Reisenfern for the present, you heard him say so."

"Then we behave toward him as to one of the honored family?"

"Certainly, certainly. What name he chooses to adopt is no business of ours. Agreed?"

"Agreed. Agreed."

"Just as well I went up," said the Graf, settling down again into his comfortable armchair under the light. "There was a sort of deputation of the senior servants, headed by Klaus, to see if I were still there. When I was, they sensibly concluded that I could not be here also, so I am some distant cousin of the family. A glass of wine, Franz, please. Very credulous people, our staff. I had reckoned on their taking me for a von Grauhugel of some kind, but it never occurred to me that they would think they were seeing a ghost in broad daylight. I mean, one doesn't. However, it's all right now."

"It is as well," said Franz, pouring the wine for his master. "If they had gone on thinking that we were ghosts—"

"They might all run away?"

"Worse than that, Herr Graf. They might have thought that we did not require food."

Chapter 4
CORDUROY TROUSERS

GEORGE WHATMORE DROVE his car up to the castle entrance just as Denmead was walking out of the great door.

"Well?" said Denmead. "How is the interesting invalid?"

"All right. He's going to London the day after tomorrow, by air, just as you said. He's bats."

"Bats? Victor? I should have said that if there was one man in the film industry with both feet firmly on the ground—in normal circumstances, that is—it was our Victor. Or do you merely mean that he is enraged at being thus incapacitated and laid low—"

"He says somebody pushed him when he fell."

" 'Who ran to push me when I fell,' " quoted Denmead. " 'Who kicked my leg to make it swell, Who often horrid lies did tell—My Brother!'"

"He says," persisted Whatmore, "that at the moment when he fell he distinctly felt a foot placed flat against the back of his waist and a hard push delivered thereby, or should it be therewith? A foot in a soft shoe of some kind, not hard at the edges."

"Very definite, isn't he? You know, George, you said yourself that Providence had pushed him down the stairs; it looks as though you were right. Did you suggest it?"

"I told him that in view of the fact that I was looking up at him from the hall below at the moment and there was no one else in sight, he could dismiss the idea. It was, I said, a muscular spasm of the nature of lumbago."

"And how did he take that?"

"Not at all well. He said he didn't harbor lumbago, and spasms he didn't go in for. He wanted me to snoop around and find out whether any of the company possessed a pair of soft shoes. Canvas things with rubber soles and flat heels, he said, was what he had in mind. Plimsolls, are they?"

"Golly!"

"Yes, quite. When I pointed out that his description would apply equally well to a man merely walking about in his socks, he turned wearily upon his pillow and gazed sadly out of the window."

"And what did you do?"

"Came away. I received the impression that I had grievously failed him."

"I gather," said Denmead, "that you had no opportunity to ask him whether he knew Reisenfern?"

"I—well, no. In any case I didn't know how to put it. We know Reisenfern isn't our man's real name and apart from shining fair hair there's nothing remarkable about his appearance and I hadn't got a photograph—" said Whatmore rather hesitantly.

"Difficult, very difficult. 'Have you ever met a fair-haired man who, if he took an assumed name, would probably call himself Reisenfern?' I understand your hesitation. Never mind, be comforted. Think how annoyed Aurea would have been if you'd come back and said Reisenfern's real name was Karl Schmidt, a chemist's assistant in Bonn, who had served a term of imprisonment for making hootch out of senna pods. I had an interview with him this morning, I thought it was time we started on him. I went up to the haunted suite and there he was, industriously studying the script."

"How was he getting on?"

"Doesn't go much on it. Says things weren't a bit like that. I told him he'd better see you and in the meantime study pages so-and-so and from here to there as we'd be taking those first."

"But, look here," said Whatmore, rather anxiously, "if he wants to start off by rewriting the script—"

"Not so bad as that, he only wants to ginger it up a bit. Less of the stately ceremonial address and a bit more pep. I thought some of his suggestions quite good. Besides, you needn't take any notice if you don't want to. Only stars of the largest size can insist on having scripts altered and he's not a star, thank goodness. They are actors, though, no doubt about that."

"Why?"

"Because Franz followed me out after the interview and touched me for a sub. He says they want to buy clothes, modern clothes. Particularly, it seems, trousers like yours. I gather that that period stuff is all they have with them. Oh, and by the way—"

"They can dress in kilts in their off-time for all I care," said Whatmore, "let alone in corduroy trousers, but why don't they just send for their baggage, wherever it is?"

"That is impossible," said Denmead. "When I asked why, Franz only grinned and repeated 'impossible.' I wondered whether they'd bolted from behind the Iron Curtain in what they stood up in and a carpetbag each."

"What, stage properties? I suppose it's possible—"

"If the Russians are producing a stage version of *Jane Eyre* or *Pride and Prejudice*. Why shouldn't they if they want to? I was going to say that Franz asked at the same time if they might borrow some modern clothes to go shopping in; their present ones might, he felt, occasion comment in Cologne. I thought he was probably right. Did you get that color filter I asked you for, in Bonn?"

"Sorry, no. I tried four shops, too. Tell you what, Denmead, we'll give these fellows a sub and I'll run them down to Cologne tomorrow. They can buy trousers while I'm hunting color filters. You'll have to lend them clothes; mine would trail on the ground behind them."

The afternoon was spent in taking the actor Reisenfern through a scene in which the Graf Adhemar was being persuaded by his mother, two uncles, and an elder sister that it was his duty to the family to marry the rich English Miss Crompton and thus reinforce the family fortunes which were, at that time, in a poor way.

"Your unfortunate father," cooed the impersonatrix of the Graf's mother, the Gräfin Beatrix, "was, as you know, unfortunate in his speculations. He wore himself out trying to recoup his losses; he died untimely from grief and anxiety. My dear son, I am sure you realize that it is incumbent upon you to step into his place and do as he would have done if he had—"

"Heaven forbid!" cried the Graf, and turned to Whatmore. "My father lost his money on the gaming tables at Monte Carlo and his health trying to cheer himself up in Paris. I mean—well, never mind. But 'do as he would have done,' I say, really, Whatmore! My mother had no illusions about him, either, and the idea of my following in his footsteps would have—"

"I am all in favor," said Whatmore, "of actors sinking themselves in their part, but when it comes to rewriting family history to suit your ideas, Reisenfern, I must say that I think that Graf Sigmund's version is more likely to be authentic."

"The Graf Sigmund? You mean that Sigmund told you this—this pretty fable? I suppose he toned it down in the interests of the family's reputation."

"He told me," said Whatmore rather stiffly, "that he had this story from his father who had it from his grandfather, a brother of the Graf Adhemar whose part you are playing."

"And nobody mentioned Paris, I suppose."

"The Graf Sigmund said that the Graf Adhemar's father went to Paris to study art."

"I believe," said the actor Reisenfern, "that Cora Pearl was indeed an object of the most undoubted art. Never mind about that. With regard to this interview we are reproducing—"

"I think we will play it as written," said Whatmore with considerable firmness. "I have, after all, engaged you as an actor, not a scriptwriter."

"Oh, very well," said the Graf. "It is not, now, a matter of the slightest importance and I apologize for interrupting. It is, after all, your play. Where did we get to?"

Whatmore was pleased with his victory and carried the two new members of his cast to Cologne the following morning with complete amiability. A spare suit of Denmead's fitted Franz not too badly, but the Graf had a good deal of slack at the top of the trousers held in by a belt.

"There is, as you might say," he remarked, exhibiting this, "room for improvement."

Whatmore drove himself and the Graf sat in the back seat, leaving Franz to sit in front beside the driver and take a sustained and intelligent interest in the car and its controls.

"But you have driven a car, I suppose," said Whatmore.

"Not such a car as this. I have, of course, driven my Herr ever since I was seventeen, but this sort of car is strange to me. Do you object to my watching you closely?"

"Not at all. On the contrary. The starter is here," Whatmore pressed a button and the engine sprang to life. "Hand brake here, and you release it thus. See? This is the clutch pedal and this is the gear lever. Four forward speeds and reverse. Bottom gear first—"

They moved off down the drive.

Whatmore should have been a schoolmaster, for he loved teaching, and Franz seemed to be an intelligent pupil. When they came out upon a stretch of level and reasonably straight road, Whatmore said: "Would you like to drive?"

Franz's face lit up. "With my Herr's permission! Mein Herr, have I your leave to try?"

"You may," said the Graf. "We can, after all, only die once."

Franz was seized with a sudden fit of coughing.

"I'll see he does no harm," said Whatmore. He pulled in to the side of the road and changed places with Franz. "Now put the hand brake off. Right off. Engage first gear, let the clutch in gently . . . . Keep close in to the side of the road."

The lesson proceeded quite well, since though Franz was plainly new to the task at least he was not nervous. Whatmore began to think him not nearly nervous enough, for once they were in top gear their progress became positively dashing.

"Here, steady on," he said. "Take it gently. A car takes more stopping, in an emergency, than you would think."

"An emergency?" said Franz. "Such as someone getting in our way? But, when I blow your tuneful horn," he did so, "the person will get out of my Herr's way. Unquestionably. They always did so."

"I don't quite understand," said Whatmore. "You say you are in the habit of driving your Herr, but you obviously don't know much about motors. What sort of a car did you have?"

"The one we most commonly used had two seats in front. Behind, there was a square compartment which could be closed down when we had the dogs with us. There were also places for the guns."

"A shooting brake?"

"Oh no. A brake is a large carriage to hold four or six persons. It has four wheels and is drawn by two strong horses. The gentlemen sit on either side, facing each other. The—"

"Horses. Drawn by horses?"

"Certainly, sir. May I address you as 'sir' since I notice your—"

"Slow down," said Whatmore sharply. "You are going much too fast considering—"

"But this is such fun," protested Franz, and put his foot hard down upon the accelerator. Whatmore leaned forward, switched off the engine, and withdrew the ignition key; the car coasted to a stop.

"But, sir—"

"Brake, please. Now then. This car in which you used to drive your Herr, what was the motive power?"

"Your pardon, sir?"

"What made it move?"

"Roland, sir, as a rule, but sometimes Gallant."

"Horses?"

"But certainly. Only one at a time, however."

"I see," said Whatmore. "Change places with me again, I think I'll drive the rest of the way."

"Certainly, sir," said Franz in a crestfallen voice. "Did I then not drive well enough to satisfy you?"

"Considering all things," said Whatmore, sliding across into the driver's seat, "I think you drove very well." He glanced into the back seat; his other passenger was comfortably reclined with his feet up and appeared to be asleep. A happy sleep, for he was definitely smiling.

Whatmore drove on into Cologne and put the car on the car-park by the Cathedral, at the back of the Dom Hotel. "I have some things to do," he said, getting out of the car. "If we meet here in an hour's time, will that suit you?"

He received no answer and looked round at his passengers to find them standing close together as if for mutual support and staring about them with a look of such extreme stupefaction as made them appear almost half-witted.

"I am so sorry," said Whatmore. "I suppose you have not been here since before the war; if I had known I would have warned you. The damage here was indeed very extensive."

"War damage," said the Graf in an undertone, and walked a few paces forward to look down toward the river over acres upon acres of pounded desolation with trees growing sparsely and here and there the jagged ruin of some corner of a house more sturdy than the rest.

"They have rebuilt the Höhestrasse," said Whatmore. "Very fine buildings, too. It's over there, look. You'll find everything you want there, I'm sure."

"Thank you," said the Graf without turning his head, but Franz threw out his arms in a wild gesture like a man thrusting away an evil dream.

"But," he said painfully, "people *lived* there."

"I'll meet you here in an hour's time," said Whatmore, and walked hastily away. He turned at a corner and glanced back; the two men still stood there like statues, unmoving.

"If they want to stand gaping instead of buying trousers, I can't help it," he muttered. "It's nearly fifteen years since we started bombing here, they must have been small boys then. I suppose Denmead's right, they have been in Poland or somewhere. Of course, that would account for the horses. There's always a rational explanation."

But when he returned, complete with the color filters Denmead wanted, he found his passengers completely restored in spirits and clothed afresh in garments of today. The Graf, in a dark green turtleneck sweater, corduroy trousers to tone, and brown shoes with incredibly thick crepe soles, was plainly very pleased with himself and, indeed, looked very well. Franz, in a neat dark suit, a white shirt with a stiff collar, and a completely subdued tie, looked exactly as a self-respecting manservant should. He also carried parcels. Whatmore congratulated them.

"We took advice," said the Graf carelessly. "We told the fellow what we wanted and he was most helpful. These clothes of mine are well enough, are they? I ventured, my dear Whatmore, to model myself on you, I hope you do not object? Most kind of you. Yes, they are most comfortable, so easy that I have a lurking fear that they may suddenly fall off and leave me in an awkward predicament. However, doubtless my fears are groundless and I shall get used to the feeling. I hope that your shopping was equally successful? Splendid, my dear fellow, splendid. It was most kind of you to bring us here. May I sit beside you for the journey home if Franz may sit behind? He can then take care of our large and burdensome parcels. Let me reassure you, Whatmore, I have no ambition to drive. We are ready, if you are?"

When they reached the castle, Franz returned, with grateful thanks, the borrowed garments and then rejoined his master in the haunted suite.

"Lunch," said Franz, "will be brought up in ten minutes."

"Glad to hear it," said the Graf. "Very odd, this urgent desire for the intake of food at least three times a day, after all these years. I suppose we use up energy, do we? There's another thing we have used up very rapidly this morning, Franz, and that is money. How much have we left?"

Franz took a handful of coins from his pocket and counted them out on the table.

"Three marks and seventy-five pfennigs."

"Oh. We shall not be able to buy very much with that. Moreover, I have only one pair of socks. I am greatly concerned that we may have spent too freely."

"Certainly not," said Franz loyally. "The Herr Graf could not possibly wear shirts of anything but silk. Besides, I was thinking over this problem on the way home and I remember that I have some money."

"You! Where did you get that from?"

"Mein Herr, principally from you though there were also a few tips. Consider, mein Herr, that you paid me well for those days and also how few expenses I had. Cigars and wine cost me little—"

"You helped yourself to mine, of course," laughed his master. "Did you think I did not know?"

"On the contrary, I assumed you did. It was always the custom then, though I learn from Klaus that in these days it is discouraged. More pay and fewer perquisites is now the rule. I was saving up, mein Herr, to buy the inn in the village here for my years of retirement. Old Koestler and his wife had no children, if you remember, which was a pity, for if they had had a daughter I could have married her and not troubled with saving."

"Suppose she had refused you?"

"Oh, mein Herr! A village girl refuse the Graf's personal servant? Impossible."

"I suppose so. I had not realized that you were so desirable a *parti*, besides, of course, your personal attributes." Franz bowed. "Those girls in Paris—"

"Let us not," broke in Franz, "rake up what is now, we may hope, forgotten." He pulled down the corners of his mouth.

"But where is this money?"

"In the orchard of the inn. I buried it in a strong iron box, just before we left the last time for Heidelberg. I was not sure whether the Herr intended to return here at once or take up his residence elsewhere."

"You were quite right. So long as my mother was alive my residence with—with my wife would definitely have been elsewhere!"

There came a knock at the door and the majordomo in person entered to supervise the service of the Graf's lunch. Klaus did not, of course, do anything himself; he merely stood there watching intently every move of the two footmen who laid the table and set the dishes without once daring to raise their eyes to the face of the man they served. They backed to the door, bowed, and edged out. Klaus, who carried in his hand a tall slim wand of office with an enameled-silver emblem on the top of it, struck it three times upon the floor and announced "The Herr is served."

"Thank you, Klaus," said the Graf Adhemar.

Chapter 5
THE IRON BOX

THE INN of the village of Grauhugel stood a little back from the road with a cobblestoned forecourt; a narrow lane ran down upon either side of it to the grounds belonging to it at the back. There was a patch of garden, producing a rather halfhearted collection of lettuce and cabbage, a small orchard immediately adjoining, and behind this a vineyard running up the hillside from which the innkeeper annually made wine for his local customers. His orchard trees were of various kinds, including some very fine cherry trees; at that time they were loaded with shining fruit.

He suffered, like other orchard owners, from small boys and had one of his own. The harvest of the year before had been a poor one throughout the district; many of his neighbors had had no cherries at all and even the innkeeper's trees were but thinly speckled with them. The result was that there had been noises in the orchard at night; scratchy noises as of small boys climbing trees and snapping noises when twigs were broken off. Then, in the morning, there would be even fewer cherries. Shouted imprecations from the bedroom window did no good and merely vexed his neighbors; by the time he had run downstairs and out across the garden there was no one there.

The innkeeper ground his teeth and looked vaguely round his kitchen for inspiration. His eye fell upon his father's bell-mouthed blunderbuss, which hung upon the wall by the fireplace with its wide mouth gaping at the ceiling. He took it down.

"Kaspar," said his wife, coming into the kitchen, "what do you do with that old thing?"

"I clean it," said the innkeeper with a grin, "and then I load it. Then we will see if I lose my cherries."

"Kaspar! To shoot—not to shoot—to shoot at—not at the children? No, no. I tell the priest, I tell the mayor—"

"Idiot," said the innkeeper, not unkindly. "I load it only with black powder and a few wads, but do not tell anyone that. A loud bang, that is all, and the wads whistling through the leaves. What? Not a word. Where is our innocent young son, the little rip?"

"Out," she said, "with some of his friends. I saw them in the carpenter's yard as I came by."

"Good. They are within earshot. Excellent."

He loaded the gun, which had at some time been adapted from a flint-lock to take percussion caps, rammed several wads down on top of the powder, put a cap on the nipple, aimed the gun at a gooseberry bush five yards off, and pulled the trigger. For a wonder, the ancient firearm responded at once with a roar which roused the village; though the innkeeper's wife had her fingers tight in both ears she yet leapt nervously in the air and knocked a jug off the dresser with a crash to the floor.

"Now see what you have made me do," but the innkeeper only grinned as there came the sound of running feet clattering upon the cobblestones. They came with a rush, first the children of the village and then their elders, to peer round the corner of the house. The innkeeper was brushing out the barrel with a bottle brush wired to a cane, and a drift of blue smoke thinned out slowly across the garden.

"My father! My father, what is this?"

"A gun, my son. Thy grandfather's old blunderbuss, but, as thou seest, it still works very well."

"But—"

"Now I reload," said the innkeeper, "and I think perhaps I lose no more cherries, eh?"

The group became a semicircle round the back door.

"But, my father, what do you load it with?"

"Swan shot, my son."

"But," said a woman of the village, "this is barbarous. Our children—"

"I have been repeatedly assured by every mother in the place," said the innkeeper pointedly, "that their own child or children has or have never set foot in my orchard. So why worry?"

"I don't believe," said a younger woman, "that that old thing could do any harm. It only makes a bang."

The innkeeper laughed. "Look at my gooseberry bush."

They looked. The wads had ripped through it, tearing off leaves and small twigs in a most impressive manner. The group recoiled.

"Excuse me, if you please," said the innkeeper. "This reloading, it requires concentration and an absence of draft." He retired indoors and shut the door after him.

He did reload the gun though he did not believe it was really necessary. Nor was it; his orchard remained unmolested through the cherry season, the plums and even the apples. The gun still hung upon its nail, loaded but not capped in case young Kaspar felt impelled to pull the trigger. The innkeeper's wife would not touch the gun for any pretext, even to dust it; it hung there all through the winter and the spring with its bell mouth turned upwards and a ball of newspaper pushed loosely into it to keep the dust out.

The next year, this year of which we speak, the cherry harvest was, generally speaking, good and the innkeeper's was excellent.

"I do not believe that they will start their games again," said the innkeeper placidly, "but, if they do, there is the gun ready. I have bought some new caps."

One night, a warm night when the moon was three quarters full, the innkeeper awoke for no particular reason unless that, the windows being open, he had heard a noise. He lay still and listened; there was a noise or, to be more accurate, a series of small sounds. He got out of bed and went to the window.

The sounds came from the orchard and were, surprisingly, more of a metallic nature. There was a definite clink of metal and the innkeeper swore under his breath.

"What is it?" said his wife, sitting up. "Not those children again?"

"Ssh! No. This is a matter upon a larger scale altogether," he said. "These are men in the orchard. I dimly saw one cross a patch of moonlight. They are gathering the fruit in pails—I go for my gun. Listen, you can hear the pails clank. On no account show a light." He tiptoed out of the room.

His wife got up and went quietly to stand by the boy's bed. He was sound asleep, but when that gun went off in the orchard two men were digging with spades borrowed from the innkeeper's tool shed.

"Franz, are you sure this is the right spot?"

"Quite sure, mein Herr. We have not yet dug deep enough, that is all."

"Unless someone else has dug deeply enough before us. Franz, if we had a pointed rod we could push it in and—"

"Here," said Franz, and his tool scraped. "I am on it. Now, it is but to get it out."

But the soil was stiff and heavy and had not been disturbed for over eighty years. Roots, from the nearer trees, were interlaced through it, stones had to be dug out. Also, the diggers impeded each other and occasionally their spades struck together.

"We shall arouse the whole village," said Franz, "if we make so much noise."

"Would that matter?" said the Graf. "If someone comes, they can do the digging and, after all, it is your money." He wiped his brow with the back of his hand.

"But would anyone believe that?"

They cleared the top of the box at last and loosened the earth round the sides.

"There is a handle on the top," said Franz. "If I pull on that and the Herr Graf were to pull at me—"

"That box is faintly familiar to me," said the Graf, looking down into the hole.

"It is yours, mein Herr. I did but borrow it and, besides, it was only standing empty in a storeroom. The key was lost"

"I remember now. Have you got hold of it? Now then. Pull!"

The box resisted and then came up an inch and slipped back. It rose again a little more—

"Pull! Hold me—"

The box rose out of its matrix into the loose hole and was lifted out and laid on the grass.

"It seems to be locked now," said the Graf, trying the hasp.

"It will be rusted in, mein—"

There came a flash from an upper window of the inn, accompanied by a perfectly appalling bang which rattled the village windows and woke every dog in the place and ninety-nine per cent of the people. Nor was the explosion otherwise blank, for small objects tore through the foliage with odd whining noises or thudded into tree trunks; one of them hit the lid of the box and ricocheted past Franz's ear with a singing sound.

"Run, Franz, run!"

They tore out of the orchard, away from the inn, over the fence into the vineyard like startled cats and along a path toward the church. As they came among houses again, windows were flung up and heads poked out.

"What was that?"

"Kaspar's gun—"

"Look! Two men running—"

"Who are they? Stop, you!"

Ahead of them a door opened on the street and suddenly the Graf pulled up.

"Franz! What idiots we are! Don't run, you fool. Vanish!"

"What? With all those people watching?"

"Into this yard, quick! Now then!"

The innkeeper's small boy awoke with a convulsive leap and found his mother's arms about him.

"Ach! O-ooh! What—what—"

"It is nothing, my son. There is nothing to fear. It is but thy father who fired off his gun at some men who were robbing the orchard. It is all over—"

"Fired—off—his—gun?"

"That is all. They—"

The innkeeper heard their voices and came into the room.

"Did that startle thee, Kaspar, boy? It startled those bad men much more, I saw them running. Wasn't that fun? Nay," as the child's face fell and his mouth opened, "there is nothing to cry about. They are gone. Hush!"

But the rounded mouth became square-cornered like a slit for letters and a most dolorous howl came out.

"Thus hast frightened the child out of his wits!" said his mother.

"I am not frightened," bellowed the boy, kicking and hitting out with his fists. "It is—boo-hoo—all my money you have shot away— ooh! Oh—"

"Thy money! What money—where?"

"I was—saving up and I put it—in the gun. I thought—it was safe there, Mother never touched it. N-now you have g-gone and fired it away— Ow! Ow!" Tears poured down his face.

His parents looked at each other.

"Perhaps we shall find it," said his mother, "in the morning. When it is daylight we will look."

The innkeeper shook his head doubtfully. "How much was there, Kasparlein?"

"Five marks—and three half marks—and nine twenty-pfennigs and four t-ten-pfennigs and eleven five-pfennigs. I'd nearly got enough and you go and bang it all away—oh!"

"But what possessed thee to put it in such a silly place?"

"Not silly. It's you that's silly to—"

"Kaspar!"

He dissolved into fresh sobs. "I didn't want you to mind it for me, I wanted to spend it myself. All at once."

"What in the world," said his mother, "didst thou want to spend all that on? Over nine marks!"

"An—an air gun—"

The innkeeper straightened up.

"It may be," he said, "that we shall find some of it in the morning. But not, I trust, enough to buy an air gun. I go now to bring in the fruit they have picked."

He went into the orchard and found no fruit, but a hole in the ground and a small but heavy iron box. After walking round it and marveling at it for some minutes he picked it up and carried it within doors. His wife was in the kitchen warming some milk for the boy.

"I shall put a spoonful of spirits in it," she said, watching the pot. "He will cry himself into a fit." She turned away, pot in hand, and saw what her husband was carrying. "What is that?"

He put it down on the table with a bump, locked and bolted the door, and drew the curtains over the windows. "They were not stealing fruit," he said in a low voice. "They were digging and this is what they dug up."

She looked at it askance. "What is in it, I wonder?"

"Money, perhaps? How should I know?"

"Is there no name on it?"

But the box was caked with earth and corroded with rust.

"One could not tell if there were." He fetched a screwdriver and tried to lever up the hasp, but it resisted. "It is locked. The blacksmith must see to it."

She poured the hot milk into a cup, added a spoonful from a bottle, and turned to go upstairs. "Whatever it is," she said, "it is not ours."

"You are right. In the morning it shall be opened in the presence of the mayor and the priest. In the meantime I bring it upstairs for the night —and I reload my gun!"

Most of the subordinate staff at the castle had been engaged from the village and came up daily. By seven in the morning the castle was buzzing with the story, by half past eight the members of the film unit had heard it too.

"Treasure-trove dug up in an orchard! What a thrill for the village!"

"It may not be treasure," said Whatmore. "I gather that they haven't opened it yet."

"I hear there's going to be a State Opening, or am I thinking of Parliament?"

"The mayor and corporation—"

"Mayors don't have corporations in Germany, they—"

"They just go on a diet, do they?"

"Can anyone go?" asked Aurea Goldie. "I'd love to see the lid come up, displaying somebody's crown jewels."

"It might," said Whatmore, "display somebody's dead baby."

"Ugh! I shan't go!" .

"No, I wouldn't, Aurea. Boxes buried in orchards don't necessarily contain treasure."

"I'll go," said Denmead, "if they'll let me in. Then I can tell you all about it. Klaus, is that right, that this box is going to be opened in public?"

"That is so, mein Herr. Does the Herr wish to see the opening of the box? It is true that he is not a resident, but I cannot think—"

"Oh! I do not wish to intrude."

"No, no. That speaks for itself," said Klaus, who liked the even-tempered Denmead. "I know the mayor well, naturally. Would the Herr care for me to ring him up and ask if the Herr's presence—"

"Oh, would you do that? Thank you so much."

Permission practically amounting to an invitation having been given, Denmead went off and returned an hour and a half later.

"Funny business," he said thoughtfully. "Very, very funny. There was quite a gathering in a big room at the inn. There was the mayor in, believe it or not, a top hat, with a sash of office transversely across his person like—"

"Philip," said Aurea.

"What?"

"Never mind the millinery. What was in the box?"

"I'm just telling you, this is all part of it. There was the priest and various other worthies in their Sunday suits and the blacksmith with a hammer and chisel. There was everything except trumpeters blowing a fanfare. When I went in—"

"Philip!"

"Wait for it, wait for it. I was led up to a place in the front row, the priest said grace—"

"What!"

"Well, he said something. The mayor signalled to the blacksmith, who approached his chisel to the hasp and dealt it a hefty wallop with the hammer. The hasp came up, but still the lid didn't open. So the blacksmith tapped at the edges with his chisel and at last the lid came up. I couldn't see anything in it from where I sat but the mayor put his hands in and brought out a bag"—Denmead gestured with his hands—"oh, about the size of a sponge bag. Just as he brought it up level with the top of the box the bag burst and what do you think fell out?"

"I could kill you," said Aurea. "What?"

"Gold. Gold coins. Gold twenty-mark and ten-mark pieces. Rather like our sovereigns and half sovereigns, only rather larger and thinner. Of course, they were roughly equivalent in the old days. The company present let out a sort of united sigh in which I admit I joined them, and then the mayor began to count the money."

"Was it all rolling about the floor?" asked Whatmore.

"No, it all fell back in the box. The mayor fished it out in handfuls and the priest stacked it up on the table in little piles of ten, sorted for size. When they'd finished, the mayor tilted the box to show the company it was empty and then they proceeded to count. There were a hundred and sixty-seven twenty-mark pieces and seventy-nine ten-mark bits, all gold. Worth, at that time in English money, a little over two hundred pounds. It looked very nice," said Denmead plaintively.

"Who does it belong to?" asked Aurea. "The innkeeper, I suppose, since it was on his land."

"They all began to discuss that and I gathered that the land is not quite what we should call freehold, though laws aren't, of course, the same here. I gathered that the castle is a sort of ground landlord or something similar. However, the question no longer arises."

"Why not?"

"You wait. Somebody asked if there was any name or mark of any kind on the box, but it was caked with dry mud and pretty badly corroded. The blacksmith produced a wire brush and the innkeeper's wife weighed in with a bowl of hot soapy water; they shut down the lid of the box and started operations on it. That was the point when the money began to disappear."

"Disappear? You mean, the company were snitching it?"

"No, I don't. There was a biggish table; the box was on one end and the money was standing in tidy little piles, as already described, toward the other end, with the mayor and the priest brooding over it. There was, oh, I should think eighteen inches of bare table between the box and the money and about the same between the money and the other end of the table. The mayor and the priest were backed up against the end wall of the room, and the front rows of the company, including me, were sitting on chairs well back from the table. I mean, if we had wanted to touch the edge of the table I think we'd have had to stand up, I doubt if we could have reached it, sitting. Well, the first thing I noticed was the priest industriously crossing himself. I didn't take much notice at first because I don't know anything about the R. C. Church, but I believe they have a lot of services at fairly frequent intervals all day. Every three hours, is it? Anyway, I thought it was perhaps time for some of the priest's private orisons and he was just quietly getting on with it. Why not?

"The next thing was a loud gasp from the mayor. He staggered back against the wall and next time somebody tells me he's seen someone's eyes come out on stalks I shall believe him. The mayor's did. He was staring at the table and the next minute everyone else was staring too. The money, little pile by little pile, was vanishing."

"What," said Whatmore, "slowly? Sliding back out of sight, or—"

"No, no. Quite suddenly, plonk. Only there wasn't any plonk. A pile was there and then it wasn't, one at a time. If you can imagine a man standing at the table picking up the little heaps one by one and dropping them into his pockets, it was like that. Only there was no man standing there."

Denmead paused to wipe his face.

"By this time, of course, we were all on our feet and there was a lot more space between us and the table than there had been. That goes for me, too. The blacksmith just stood there with his wire brush in his hand and didn't move at all. There were about three piles left when one of the coins was dropped. Or fell down, if you prefer it. It fell on the floor just in front of me and stood up on its edge spinning, as coins do sometimes when you drop them. The next second it stopped spinning and vanished, too. I mean, you would have sworn that someone put his foot on it. Only there wasn't a foot.

"Well, the moment they'd all disappeared there was an absolute babble of chatter. It started off, as a howl and more or less kept it up, everyone talking at the top of his voice except the priest, who appeared to be talking to himself, the blacksmith, who resumed his scrubbing, and me. I mean, I was only a visitor and it wasn't my pigeon. I would have come away only I couldn't get to the door. This went on for some minutes, I don't know how long, when I noticed that the blacksmith seemed to have

found something. He scrubbed a bit more in one place, rinsed the dirt off
with a rag, and pointed out the result to the mayor. The priest left off
praying, if that was what he was doing, and shuffled along to have a look
too. The talk died down and there was absolute silence again till the mayor
took off his glasses and looked up.

" 'Gentlemen,' he said. `There are some arms engraved upon this
box, those of the highborn family von Grauhugel.' "

"What happened after that?" asked Aurea.

"I don't know. I thanked everybody for the lovely party and came
away."

The Graf and his servant also came away; just as none saw them
come, none saw them go. Denmead, striding back to the castle, passed
them by the church and did not even turn his head, though they were
within a yard of him.

"I like that man," said the Graf suddenly. "He has an honest mind.
Franz, since we are here, let us go in and look at whatever they have set
over what are rightly called our mortal remains. My generation did make
such a fuss—*Herrgott!* Not that one!"

That one was a large and ornate memorial—Victorian Gothic with
fretted pinnacles—having a canopy over it upon four twisted pillars, to
the memory of the *hochwohlgeboren* Graf Adhemar Hildebrand von Grauhugel, who by a fatal accident passed untimely to the company of his
ancestors on June 14, 1869, aged twenty-two. There followed what must
have been an exhaustive list of his virtues, since he seemed to have had
them all.

At the foot there were added a few lines to the memory of Franz
Bagel, aged twenty-three, in boyhood a companion and later the faithful
servant of the said Graf, who died attempting to save his master and here
rests with him in peace as his courage and fidelity deserve.

"It is very handsome, mein Herr," said Franz. "It must have been
very costly. "

"But I still do not like it, Franz. It is more like a piece of confection-
ery at a dinner party than a memorial. All those little pinnacles—"

"It lists most faithfully all the Herr's virtues," said Franz gravely.

"Including a large number I never had. Piety, for example, sobriety,
and prudence. Prudence, ha! Who composed that nonsense, I wonder?
The only sense in the whole silly inscription is in what it says about you.
Never mind, it's too late to alter it now. We, at least, do not have to look
at it."

Chapter 6
BLACK MARKET

THE FILM PRODUCTION proceeded upon its tortuous way. The actor Reisenfern almost left off arguing about the story, the décor, the characters, and the scenes and only suggested certain modifications in the dialogue which were so obviously improvements that they were usually adopted. Reisenfern appeared surprised to find out how hard everyone worked; he had at first treated the whole business as though it were an elaborate parlor game, "like his charades at Christmas," snorted Whatmore, but once production was really under way Reisenfern was as punctual and hard-working as Whatmore himself and a great deal more patient. Scenes were taken over and over again until Whatmore was satisfied; other members of the cast growled among themselves and said the fellow couldn't make up his mind what he did want, but the actor Reisenfern merely smiled and did what he was told. Even Whatmore noticed it.

"You are very good," he said, at the end of a rather trying day. "You must find all this repetition tiresome, especially when it is not you who are at fault."

"My dear fellow," said Reisenfern, "pray do not apologize. Most of my fellow workers are experienced in this sort of acting, I gather, from what they say. You, on the other hand, have you actually been head producer before? No, I thought not. They think they know more about it than you; they do not subordinate their wills to yours, do they? Always the little tussle, so tiring. Never mind, you will win in the end. Perseverance is all."

"Thank you," said Whatmore with a slight gasp.

Denmead had been almost too busy to eat until at last there came a slack day when arrears of film were being processed and the company were given a holiday. Most of them went up the Rhine on a steamer, leaving the castle Grauhugel in an odd state of suspended animation; Denmead spent most of the day in a long chair on the terrace where Klaus came out at intervals and ministered to him.

"Where is everybody?" asked Denmead in the middle of the afternoon. "The Herr Reisenfern?"

"The Herr and his servant have gone to Cologne. I believe the Fräulein Goldie is in her room, resting. The Herr Whatmore has gone for a walk. Would the Herr care for a cup of coffee? And, perhaps, cakes?"

Denmead thought it an excellent idea; Klaus gave the order and superintended the service.

"It is very beautiful here," said the Englishman.

"It is, indeed," said Klaus.

"A fine castle."

"We think so," said Klaus with a smile. "No doubt there are many larger and finer, but this is ours." He nodded to the footman, who retired.

"So old," pursued Denmead, "and yet so complete. One feels it ought to have a ghost."

"But it has, *gnä'* Herr. It is said that in times long past there were several, notably a white lady who walked up and down the great stairway, but she has not been seen for very many years. Even my grandfather never saw her. Now there is only the Graf Adhemar."

Denmead's ears seemed to prick up of their own accord.

"Have you ever seen him?"

Klaus laughed indulgently. "We have all seen him, *gnä'* Herr, since he was drowned eighty-six years ago. We of the staff are accustomed to see him; he was much beloved in life and we are—how shall I say it—we are glad he is still with us. Still part of our lives, our young Graf Adhemar Hildebrand. We are proud of him, you understand."

"I begin to understand. And in the village, do they believe in him too?"

"Believe in him? One believes what one sees with one's eyes, *gnä'* Herr. During eighty years very many of the village people have served here; they still do. The Herr may have seen them coming and going, and in the old days when there was much entertaining, many more of them did so. The Herr Graf walks about the castle at night, mein Herr, not every night but very often. If we meet him we stand back respectfully to let him pass as we did when he was in life; sometimes he looks at us and seems pleased and sometimes he smiles. It is all quite natural and pleasant, *gnä'* Herr, when one has known it all one's life."

"I suppose so. Yes, I can see that it would be."

"When we were little children our parents told us about him and when we grew older we saw him ourselves. Let me pour the Herr another cup of coffee and these cakes are good, the ones with the cream on the top."

"There is a suite here, I think the Herr Reisenfern has it," said Denmead. "It is called the haunted suite, is it not?"

"It is. A stupid name; I myself and the upper servants never call it that. Its proper name is the Graf Adhemar's suite. It is because the Herr Graf is sometimes seen there that it is called haunted, but that is no reason to apply that word to it. It—how shall I put it—there is something unnatural and alarming about haunting. It would make one creep a little, yes?

There is nothing unnatural about our Herr Graf. He is part of our lives."

"Yes, of course. I see that perfectly. So long as the Herr Reisenfern does not mind—"

Klaus appeared, without having moved, to have retired a little distance.

"I have not heard, mein Herr, that the Herr Reisenfern has complained at all."

"No, no. Nor have I. The Herr Reisenfern is quite extraordinarily like some of the family portraits, and he told us that Reisenfern was not his real name. I have sometimes wondered whether he was a connection of the family."

"I could not say, mein Herr. There are many connections of the high-born family."

"No doubt. I did not wish to appear inquisitive, please believe me. The Herr's identity is his own business entirely. You are quite right, these cakes are extraordinarily good."

"Thank you, *gnä'* Herr. I will tell the cook, who will be gratified. Now, if the *gnä'* Herr will excuse me, I have duties—" Klaus smiled and backed away.

"Of course," said Denmead cordially, "and thank you for your pleasant company."

Klaus said that the honor was his and went away. Denmead lit a pipe and sat looking away over the treetops to the blue distance which hid the Rhine.

"Yes, I see," he murmured after a time, "but even that doesn't explain how and why the money vanished."

In the meantime the Herr Reisenfern and his servant had, indeed, gone to Cologne.

When the hundred and sixty-seven gold twenty-mark pieces and the seventy-nine gold ten-mark pieces had been safely transferred from the inn to the Graf's suite at the castle, they were spread out upon a table and the Graf and his servant looked at them.

"Lock the door, Franz."

Franz did so.

"I think we will put these away behind that panel, if it still works. Try it, will you? The opening ceremony this morning was so public that everyone will hear about it and if these coins are seen lying about here it might occasion comment and the comment might reach the ears of the English. I do not wish to reveal myself to the English. What is the matter, has the panel stuck?"

"It is a little stiff," said Franz, working away at a square of the paneled wall behind the door. "There, it has opened at last. I will soap the
slides. The Herr Denmead was present at the inn this morning."

"I saw him, it could not be helped." The Graf smiled. "We are not very
experienced ghosts, Franz. If we had dematerialized last night instead of
losing our heads and running home, we could have picked up the box complete, as we did the money this morning, and brought it away with us."

"That would have been a pity, by permission. Consider, mein Herr,
what a treat for the village to see that! They will talk about it for years;
when they are old men sitting in chimney corners they will tell the story
to generations yet unborn. How nice for them, mein Herr, to have such a
story to tell!"

"You may be right. Now let us put the money away and then you can
make the slide work more—there is something at the back of the cupboard, Franz, what is it?"

"I do not know, Highborn," said Franz, dropping suddenly into the
formal address. The Graf crossed the room and took from the back of the
small, deep cupboard a wisp of fine material. It had once been white but
was now yellow with age and gray at the folded edges with dust; when it
was unfolded it was seen to be a delicate lawn handkerchief, large by
today's standards but incredibly fine.

"I remember now," said the Graf as one talking to himself. "I had it
from her the last time I left her in Heidelberg, the last time before I went
back for our wedding. She said I was a robber, I had stolen her heart and
now I must have her handkerchief too. Cecilie, my wife. Franz, you remembered that it was there?"

"When I saw it, Highborn," said Franz with his eyes on the floor, "I
remembered."

"It is well," said the Graf, folding the handkerchief and putting it into
his breast pocket. "Perhaps it will not be long, now, Cecilie, my wife . . .
Franz, I will be very patient and obedient to all that this Englishman says;
what does it matter if his story is full of blunders? Then I may be permitted to set matters right and have done with waiting. Let us put the money
away quickly, someone may come."

The sliding panel was finally closing when there came a knock at the
door.

"The Herr Whatmore's compliments. He awaits the Herr Reisenfern
in the courtyard."

"Good. I come. Come, Franz, and do not let us keep the Herr waiting,
he is anxious to get on and so am I."

As has been said, considerable progress was made in the next few days, helped on by the actor Reisenfern's new docility, and it was not until the rest day came that anything more could be done about the money.

"Mein Herr," said Franz, "by permission, they do not use money like this in these days. Those paper notes, such as the Herr Whatmore advanced us to buy our clothes, are all the mode."

"What do you mean? It cannot be that those gold coins are now no good?"

"On the contrary, they are much more good. There was talk in the servant's hall of what each one would have done with the gold coins if they had had them and each one began in the same way. To change the gold into paper marks, one gets three or more times their value."

"What? Are you sure you heard right? What, sixty or seventy marks for a twenty-mark piece? Why?"

"Because gold is more valuable than paper," said Franz simply, and this was so obviously true that the Graf believed him at once.

"We take them to a bank, I assume," he said.

"Not a bank, mein Herr. I do not know why, but it seems that banks do not deal with this sort of exchange, they only pay out mark for mark. No good at all."

"Then what—"

"There are certain men in Cologne who deal in this. They are to be found near the Cathedral. They have a password, I have had it all explained to me very clearly. They stand about and we also stand about. Then, after a little, one of them comes up and asks if we have anything to sell. That is the password, 'anything to sell.' Then we say, 'What price for gold Doppelkronen?' or 'for gold kronen' if it is the ten-mark pieces we sell. Then they offer a price and we take it or not as we see fit."

"It is all very mysterious," said the Graf. "Passwords? I suppose they are a guild."

"That is so, I believe. It is called the black market."

"Very strange. I have heard of cattle markets, corn markets and flower markets, but this black, what is it?"

"The name of the guild," said Franz unhesitatingly.

"Oh, very well. Let us go into Cologne and see how we fare with your black marketeers. You can do the chaffering, you appear to be the expert in these matters. I do not remember ever discussing the price of anything in all my life."

"Of course not. It would not be fitting."

"No. Shall we take it all, Franz, at once? Or try a part of it first? We do not wish to embarrass the guild."

Eventually they took fifty coins of each denomination done up in little packets of ten. They came out of Cologne Station, strolled round behind the Cathedral, and stood about looking at nothing in particular. Franz's information proved to be correct; before many minutes had elapsed a man strolled up to them and said, out of the corner of his mouth, "Anything to sell?"

The Graf stepped back and left the negotiations to Franz, who assumed that he ought to imitate the guild manner.

"Gold coins," he said obliquely. "Doppelkronen."

"What?" said the man. "Gold twenty-mark pieces?"

"That's right. How much?"

"Depends on the weight. Are they thin?"

"Thin?"

"Old, worn coins. They——"

"These," said Franz impressively, "are as new from the mint. What price?"

The Graf, who had been looking the man over, caught Franz by the sleeve and drew him back.

"Not too many at once," he murmured. "We have no means of knowing whether this fellow is a genuine member of the Black Market Guild——"

"He had the password," objected Franz.

"That is so, but he looks a rogue to me."

"I will be careful," said Franz, and turned back to the man, who said: "Sixty-five marks, if they are as you describe. How many have you got?"

The Graf nudged Franz, who said: "Ten."

"Let me look at them." Franz stared at the man coldly until he added: "If you please."

"That is better," said Franz. The Graf passed one of his little packets to Franz, who unrolled it and showed the coins in the palm of his hand.

"You are right," said the man, peering at them. "They are as fresh from the mint. Where did you dig those up?"

"In the orchard," said Franz without hesitation, and the man broke into a laugh.

"All right! I deserved that for asking. Six hundred and fifty marks." He took out his wallet, which seemed to be full of money, and counted out the sum into Franz's other hand in ten- and twenty-mark notes, rather creased and grubby. The Graf's nostrils twitched and the man, who noticed most things, noticed this also.

"What's the matter with your friend? Doesn't he like the smell of money?"

"Here is your gold," said Franz, and gave it to him. "We may, perhaps, meet again."

"If you find any more like that in the orchard, come and tell me."

"Do you buy ten-mark pieces also?" asked Franz.

"Certainly, when I can get them. At half the price, naturally. Thirty-two marks fifty, if they are as good as these."

"We may see you again," said Franz, and turned to follow the Graf, who had moved away.

"Make it soon," said the black marketeer. "There's still some stuffing in my wallet, as you saw."

"Let us go to some café," said the Graf when they were out of ear-shot, "and take a little wine. I am not sure of those dirty notes; are you satisfied that they are good? If we pay with one of them the tapster will soon tell us if they are spurious. I cannot understand how, in printing money on paper, they can ensure that any printer cannot copy them."

"These matters are beyond my knowledge," admitted Franz, "but surely such an act would be punishable? The man would know that we should denounce him to his guild."

"I daresay that you are right, but we will make sure."

However, the notes appeared to be quite good. The Graf and Franz ordered half a bottle of wine between them.

"No, sit at my table, Franz. I wish to discuss this matter."

"But it is not fitting! That I should sit at the same—"

"Sit down!"

Franz, red to the hair with quite genuine embarrassment, lowered himself gingerly on to the very edge of the chair.

"And try not to look as though the seat were red-hot! About this money, shall we change some more?"

Franz muttered something about its being as the Graf commanded.

"Franz! Will you stop being stupid? Sit back in your chair. Right back. Now pick up your glass and drink from it. That's right. And do try not to look as though I were torturing you. Now, then. What about the money? Idiot, dunderhead, have you forgotten that it is yours anyway?"

Franz looked across the table and suddenly his face split into a wide grin.

"Indeed, mein Herr, I had, but does it matter? It is only how much we shall want. The Herr will wish to reward the servants—"

"And you want—"

"A bicycle, Herr Graf."

"A— What did you say?"

"A bicycle. That is the name of those shining metal machines with two wheels; one sits upon it and propels it by pushing pedals with one's feet—there. There is one passing at the moment."

"Yes, I see. I have, indeed, seen several of them since we came back. There are even one or two in the village. Certainly you shall have one, Franz, but what for?"

"Mein Herr, a—a—an embarrassment. A foolish thing, but—"

"If it embarrasses you it must indeed be something remarkable. Tell me, Franz."

Franz took another sip of his wine and looked down at his hands.

"Since the Graf commands. The other evening, after my Herr had dispensed with my services, I went down to the village and met a girl—"

"You always did. Continue."

"She was both pretty and pleasant to talk to. We strolled down to the bridge, talking together; she told me about her family, her brothers and sisters. When we reached the bridge we leaned on the parapet to look down at the water; when she leaned forward, a locket, which she was wearing round her neck, swung forward and I made some remark about it. She showed it to me and said that her great-grandmother, now dead, had given it to her. Mein Herr, I recognized the locket."

"Oh dear," said the Graf sympathetically.

"Mein Herr, it is one of those which open easily if you know how to do it, a part slides sideways and then the locket opens—the Herr knows? Yes. When I was but seventeen I was much attracted to Lieschen, she was a little older than I and very serious. I bought her the locket and put a piece of my hair inside, but I did not tell her that nor show her how to open it. I was, if the Herr will believe it, shy in those days. At least, with her."

"Some women," nodded the Graf, "have that effect upon one."

"She married the miller and I thought I was brokenhearted. I soon found I was not, but I am still glad that I did not show her the trick of the locket. The other night this girl took it off to show me and I opened it for her; the hair was still inside."

"She was surprised?"

"Yes, mein Herr. I told her I had seen lockets like that before. She said the hair was like mine, the same color exactly. I gave her back the locket and took her home to her mother and therefore, mein Herr, I should like to have a bicycle."

"Because—?"

"Because, if I go further afield I may see a girl whose face and manner please me without discovering that ninety years ago I adored her greatgrandmother."

"I see your point," said the Graf thoughtfully. "You shall have your bicycle."

"I thank the Herr," said Franz.

"What do they cost?"

"I have no idea."

"We will change another ten gold pieces. Let us see if our former friend is still about. I misjudged him, thinking he might pay us in false notes."

They went back to the spot where they had met him earlier and looked about.

"I do not see him—yes, there he is. I was very wrong, Franz, to think him a rascal; there he is talking to two policemen."

The Graf and his servant walked up to the little group. Their former acquaintance did not look pleased to see them or, indeed, as though he had ever seen them before, but the Graf was anxious to atone for his former mistrust and did not notice.

"Mein Herr, please excuse our breaking in upon you with your friends. We have some more gold pieces we should like to s—"

The man broke in with a howl of anguish and the policemen pounced.

"So it's you," they said, "who sold gold pieces to this man? Good, we've been waiting for you. You're coming to the station."

The Graf drew himself up.

"My good fellows," he said haughtily, "we will go to the station when we have occasion for your services, not before. We—"

"Cheese it," said the police, or words to that effect. At that moment a police van, which had been summoned by telephone, drew up alongside and threw open its hospitable doors. The Graf, his servant, and the black marketeer were hustled inside, the doors slammed, and the van swirled away.

"What in the devil's name did you do that for?" asked the man angrily. "I'd just told them those Doppelkronen was found in a box under the bed when my granny died and you have to blow along and—"

"I have not the faintest idea," said the Graf loftily, "what you are talking about."

"All right. You say your piece about digging them up in the orchard and see what you get."

"Silence, fellow," said the Graf Adhemar von Grauhugel.

Chapter 7
THE HAWKER

THE POLICE VAN rolled up to the police station, the prisoners were extracted from it and whisked inside to stand in a row in front of the Station Sergeant's desk while their misdeeds were recited and written down in a book. The black marketeer kept his eyes on the floor, scowling; Franz looked straight in front of him, and the Graf, adopting the easy pose of one set apart by nature from personal indignity, set one hand upon his hip and looked out of the window.

When the recital was ended the police asked the black marketeer for his name and address; when he told them they laughed scornfully and asked whether he had been born again since the time when his name was so-and-so—something quite different from the one he had just given—with an address in München Gladbach. The prisoner said that the police were confusing him with someone else and under cover of the argument Franz and his master exchanged a few words.

"Franz. Should we vanish?"

"Better not, here in public. Let me answer them."

Accordingly, when the police left questioning the spiv and turned their attention to Franz, he gave the names of Karl Schweiz and Jakob Meister for himself and the Graf and said that they had come up for the day from Düesseldorf, where they had spent their hitherto blameless lives. As for the gold, it was their own and they had no idea that it was wrong to sell it.

"The taller one," said the police who had arrested them, "said that he had some more."

"Search them," said the Station Sergeant, but the Graf said with exquisite if acid politeness that he would not give them that trouble, and emptied his pockets upon the Sergeant's desk. One of the police ran his hands over the Graf to make sure that that really was all and that he carried no weapons. Franz allowed himself, without protest, to be searched and the police found the balance of the six hundred and fifty marks; these and the gold coins were put away inside the Sergeant's desk after having been counted.

"Thirty Doppel-kronen and fifty kronen in gold," said the Sergeant. "You agree that is correct?"

"That is correct," said the Graf.

"That is a large number of gold coins for any man to own in these days," said the Sergeant. "Where did you get them from?"

"Nowhere. They are mine and always have been."

"Indeed," said the Sergeant skeptically. "Put these men in the cells, that fellow by himself and these two together. Not for years," he added to his clerk as the prisoners were led away, "have I seen so many gold coins all at once. An odd one here and there, on a watch chain perhaps, but ninety all at once, no. Pass me that tin box, it will keep them together."

"Should they not," suggested the clerk, "go in the safe?"

"They shall, presently, be sure of that." Two cell doors clanged shut down a passage behind the charge-room and the police constables returned.

"They gave no trouble," they said.

"They'd better not," said the Sergeant. He closed his desk, locked it, and went on with his work; the constables went out again into the streets and the clerk returned to his entries.

The Graf and his servant waited in the cell until they were reasonably sure of not being interrupted and then slowly and rather laboriously dematerialized.

"I suppose it is possible, with practice," said the Graf, "to do this as suddenly as blowing out a candle, but I find it needs great concentration."

"Let the Herr take his own time," urged Franz. "I did it suddenly last night and it turned me giddy. Anyone observing me would have said I was drunk."

"The odd thing," said the Graf, "is the difficulty I find in being quite certain I am completely gone from sight. It is tiresomely easy to remain a barely perceptible shimmer. I saw myself in a glass two nights ago and I was horribly startled. I think we are all right now, let us go outside. I do not like this place, the atmosphere is sordid to the last degree."

"Completely unsuitable," agreed Franz, "for my Herr's distinguished presence." From habit he sprang to the door to open it and fell through it, ejaculating "Ach!"

"That is the first time that I have ever known you to pass through a doorway before me. Idiot," as Franz began to apologize, "I cannot describe how funny you looked. Never mind it, let us go out."

On the pavement outside the police station the inaudible discussion continued.

"We learn continually, Franz. We know now that it is illegal to sell gold coins. I cannot understand why, but there it is. Nor can I subscribe to its being a crime."

"It is some stupid new law," said Franz, almost in tears with mortification, "and it was I who misled the Herr Graf into this."

"Let it be, it is of no importance. But I do not see why they should retain our money. Let us go in and get it."

The Sergeant went on with his work and the clerk uninterruptedly added up columns of figures. Even the half-dozen flies revolving round the ceiling light continued their mysterious circuits, but the tin box in the desk was empty and Franz's packet of notes was once more in his possession.

"That is better—" he began, but the Graf cut him short.

"It is not better. We have now not only our own money but that of your black marketeer. I brought it away with the idea of returning it to him; I thought to take his wallet to him in his cell, but that is of no use, they will only take it from him again."

They considered the matter.

"There is only one thing to do," said the Graf, "and that is to get the man out also. It is true that he is a rogue, but it was at least partly our fault that he is there. I could not reconcile it with my position to leave him to bear the whole brunt of our offenses."

"No, mein Herr."

"When we get him outside here we shall have to get him away quickly, since he cannot vanish as we can." The Graf looked about him; there was an open car parked close to them just outside the police station entrance. In point of fact it was the private car of the Commissioner of Police, who was within the building. "Can you drive that vehicle, Franz?"

Franz went to look at it, particularly the controls. "I think so, mein Herr. It is sufficiently like the Herr Whatmore's in many respects, such as clutch pedals, accelerators, starting facilities—"

"Spare me," said the Graf. "Now then. We simply go through, seize him by the arms, run him through the office, and cast him into the back seat of this vehicle. If we are quick they will be too surprised to stop us. I will leap into the back and reassure him while you drive away. It does not matter which way you go so long as it is rapidly from here."

The black marketeer was sitting dolefully in his cell, heaping ingenious curses upon the heads of those two idiots who had no more sense than to walk up and announce, in the hearing of two policemen, that they had "some more gold" to sell. Just as he was telling that perfectly credible story about the box under his granny's bed and the police were, at least, listening. He was, of course, on his way to the bank to pay it in— Some sudden, irresistible force—it felt like hands on his arms—lifted him to his feet; he was just about to cry out when he was violently propelled the length of the cell and slammed against the door with a thud which almost winded him besides banging his head painfully. He fetched his breath with an effort and yelled with terror.

"Provoking," said the Graf. "I had completely forgotten he could not pass through as we can."

The Sergeant, hearing the yell, which was immediately followed by others like it, jumped to the natural conclusion that the two prisoners encaged together were fighting. He sprang to his feet, buckled round him the belt which carried the cell keys upon the end of a strong chain, and set off down the passage to quell the disturbance. He was a stout and sturdy man, accustomed to dealing with the refractory; the clerk merely looked up with a grin and did not offer to accompany him.

"Let me out!" yelled the voice. "Let me out of here!"

Since the only openings between the cells and the passage were small gratings in the steel doors, the Sergeant could not tell exactly from which cell the noise came. Besides, he thought he knew. He came first to that in which had been confined the two prisoners together and kicked the door before looking in through the grating.

"Stop that noise at once or I'll—"

His voice died away as he perceived without belief that the cell was empty. The Sergeant's hand, with the keys on the end of their chain, came up to unlock the door when, by some unseen agency, they were plucked from his hand and the key inserted into the lock of the next door instead. Since he was literally attached to the key this involved his going with it in a sideway stagger like a momentary giddiness.

The black marketeer's cell door came open and swung back toward the Sergeant, who instinctively tugged at the chain so sharply that it tilted the key in the lock and jammed it there. Also, some oppression seemed to be holding him back when he wished to leap forward.

The prisoner came out; not willingly, as prisoners usually leave their cells, but with a plain reluctance expressed by his clinging first to the doorpost and then to the door, but both in vain. He came out in a series of jerks as a worm emerges from the turf when a thrush has found it; he passed within a foot of the Sergeant, who was powerless, as in a nightmare, to raise his hands. The prisoner proceeded along the passage leaning backward from the feet upward; an impossible angle only attained in the ordinary way by novice skaters who, having lost control of their skates, are about to assault the ice with the backs of their heads. Nevertheless, he passed by. The Sergeant, finding himself free of his inexplicable restraint, sprang after him only to find himself brought up short, like a leaping yard dog, by the limits of his chain.

In the charge-room the clerk, who, after all, was also a member of the Force, rose at the call of duty and hurled himself at the fugitive only to find himself bounced back like a rubber ball from the nursery floor. He fell over his chair, which fell with him, and they rolled together into a corner.

The Sergeant, using words which he had forgotten he knew, managed to free himself by unbuckling the key belt. He rushed down the passage, across the charge-room, and out upon the street in time to see the Commissioner's car driven jerkily but rapidly away. There did not appear to be anyone in the driver's seat but presumably the fellow was crouched down; in any case it was difficult to see the driver on account of the odd behavior of the prisoner, who was rising and falling in the back seat. He would climb up until he was waist-high above the folded hood and seemed about to cast himself over the back, then suddenly he would slide down out of sight only to rise again. He reminded the Sergeant of a seal in the zoo, and the car passed from sight.

There was a certain man who made a living by selling souvenirs to tourists, mainly little casts of Cologne Cathedral, off a tray slung from a strap round his neck. He lived about five miles outside Cologne since the housing shortage there is still painfully acute, and drove in every day in a shabby car so decrepit that when it went it creaked and too often it would not go at all. On this day he was hours late because it refused to start; being no mechanic he was burning up his profits in repair fees. The car was well covered by insurance; if only the wretched thing would catch fire or someone would crash into it without hurting him, he would collect the money for a down payment on a new Volkswagen.

He parked it, close behind a heavy lorry, on one of the quays by the river, loaded up his tray, and got out. He was near to one of the landing stages at which the Rhine passenger steamers put in; one of them was coming in at the moment and there was a small crowd waiting to board it. Possible customers. He walked briskly away toward them.

A minute later there was a quite astonishing crash behind him, one or two women screamed, and the hawker spun round. Another car, an open one, had come up behind his own and rammed it squarely against the lorry. The hawker's car, aged and tottering, made no attempt to resist this final onslaught of fate but rose up in the middle like a bent hairpin and disintegrated, scattering models of Cologne Cathedral about itself like confetti in carnival time. There were some horrid squeaks and groans and the whole group settled down as immobile as the statue of the Laocoön and nearly as inextricably entangled.

The hawker and some of the men in the crowd ran toward the crash with unpleasant visions of a dead driver somewhere in the wreckage. Only one man, however, came to view as they approached and he seemed to be quite unhurt, probably because he had been travelling in the back seat of the open car. He rose to his full height, stepped upon the seat, leapt down into the road, and ran for it, toward the steamer. The hawker knew him as one of the illicit traders who hang about the Cathedral square and spoke to him as he passed.

"Are you hurt?"

"Lend me some money," said the black marketeer, pausing in his flight. "I've lost my wallet."

"What's that," said the hawker, pointing, "sticking out of your pocket?"

"Oh—so it is—I didn't—" The black marketeer ran on, across the quay, up the gangway to the steamer, and out of sight. The hawker raised his eyebrows and went on to inspect the wreck.

"There's nobody here," said one of the men, stooping and peering.

"Must have jumped in time," said another. "And run away. Whose car is this scrap iron in the middle?"

"Mine," said the hawker. "What I want to know is, who does the other belong to?"

"I can tell you that," said a third man. "It's the Commissioner of Police's, that's who."

The hawker made no comment, but within his breast his heart was singing.

At the police station the Commissioner of Police, who had heard his car start up, looked out of the window too late to see anything but its tail vanishing behind a bus. He galloped down the stairs, breathing slaughter, and met the Sergeant in charge staggering in at the door.

"That's my car—who's taken it? All stations call—radio all peter-cars—"

The Sergeant pulled himself together and did so while the Commissioner looked angrily about him and saw, down the passage, a cell door standing open with the key in the lock, a chain hanging from the key, and a belt hanging from the chain.

"What's been going on here? What are you playing at? Is this a police station or a madhouse?"

"I think it's a madhouse, sir," said the Sergeant simply.

"What—what—You!" to the clerk; "get out!"

The clerk fled, shutting the door behind him, and the Commissioner proceeded with his inquiry. When he heard that three prisoners were missing as well as his car he turned purple; when the Sergeant tried to describe how the evasion had been made, words almost failed his hearer, but not quite.

After some time, during which the Sergeant merely stood at attention saying, "Yes, sir," and "No, sir," alternatively, the Commissioner eventually ran down and ceased, and there was silence.

"At least," ventured the Sergeant, "I've got all their money." He unlocked his desk and threw the lid back. "It is in this tin box—" His voice trailed off and the Commissioner, who had sunk into a chair, got up to look.

"I really don't know," he said in a comparatively mild voice, "whether to throw you into one of the cells or send for a doctor."

"Yes, sir," said the Sergeant.

"Yes what?"

"I mean, I don't know either, sir."

"This cock-and-bull story," began the Commissioner—-

On the desk in front of him a piece of paper came to rest, still quivering slightly and with a tendency to curl up at the edges. It was a piece of the official police paper with a printed heading; there was a stock of it upon the clerk's table across the room. There was writing upon it and the two men stooped to read it.

"To pay," it said, "for the damaged chariots."

At the far end of the Sergeant's desk there was a flat tin tray for letters, labeled IN. It had been empty, but even as the men raised their eyes from the note there was a clatter as a cascade of gold coins fell into it. Three cascades, to be correct, as though a man were emptying his pockets in handfuls. The Commissioner leaned heavily upon the desk and stared with bolting eyes, but the Sergeant was long past being surprised at anything.

"There, sir," he said, indicating the largesse with a careless wave of the hand, "you see the kind of thing I mean?"

The Graf and his servant went back to the railway station.

"It seemed the right thing to do," said the Graf. "We did, after all, cause a great deal of damage and, in any event, it seems difficult to exchange those coins to advantage."

"But we can still exchange them normally at the bank," said Franz. "Would it—it is for the Herr to say—would it meet with the Herr's approval if I were to take driving lessons?"

"I think you would do better to take riding lessons, Franz. On a bicycle."

Chapter 8
THE DUEL

THE FILM STORY which Whatmore and his friend the Graf Sigmund had worked out between them was not so much a biography of the late lamented Graf Adhemar Hildebrand as a highly embroidered cloak hung upon the shoulders of a figurehead called by his name. It was, indeed, founded upon fact, but as everyone knows, foundations are but a small fraction of a finished building and mostly out of sight.

It started with the Graf as a small boy with a tutor and Franz as a small boy in attendance; these scenes had already been shot with two boy actors and were safely "in the can." When the Graf was about eighteen he went, still with Franz at his heels, to the University of Heidelberg. This was perfectly true, but, if he really lived the sort of life which the film depicted, one wonders when he found any time to study. Perhaps he did not, for Adhemar von Grauhugel was not of the studious type, but it was the accepted idea for such as he to spend two or three years at Heidelberg.

There was, in the outskirts of Bonn, a deserted film studio which had been used by the Germans during the war for the making of propaganda films. It was somewhat out of repair, but the Whatmore film company did not need to use much of it; the essential fittings were still more or less there and a week or two of intensive work by Whatmore, Denmead, and a few others had brought it to an adequate standard. A few simple sets representing students' rooms, a lecture room, a tavern interior, and so forth, provided, at little cost, all that Whatmore needed.

The Graf Adhemar had studied the script with commendable attention and had, therefore, read the tavern scenes where the innkeeper's daughter brings round the steins—tall stoneware mugs—of beer to the Graf and his fellow students amid laughter, badinage, and song. He raised his eyebrows and looked at Franz as though about to comment, then changed his mind and read the pages through again in silence.

"Tomorrow," said Whatmore one evening, "we will start working at that Bonn studio on some of those tavern scenes. Not the ones with the innkeeper's daughter, she won't be here till next week, but we ought to get through most of the rest of them in a few days. I have got some of the students from Bonn University to come out as extras. I picked out men who can sing and all they have to do is to lounge about, drink beer, and join in the choruses."

"That should not be difficult," said the Graf. "That is what they do, in any case, normally, unless students have changed a great deal since I was a student myself."

"I shouldn't think so," said Whatmore; "it can't be so long since you were a student. Where were you?"

"At Heidelberg."

"Oh, were you? I don't think the Heidelberg student scenes are far wrong, are they? The Graf Sigmund helped me a lot with those, he was there himself. You would have been up with him, would you—no, you're too young. He is an older man than you."

"I was not there at the same time as Sigmund," agreed the Graf Adhemar. "About those scenes with—"

"By the way, I wanted to make it quite clear about your songs. When you are acting, on the set, the scenes where you are singing, I don't want you really to sing."

"I beg your pardon?"

"The point is this. When people are really singing with all their hearts, it may sound very nice but, if you notice, they do tend to make the most extraordinary grimaces. Quite ugly, actually."

The Graf thought for a moment and then smiled. "You are quite right. I remember a soprano in Paris—pretty woman, too—when she took a top note it was like my grandmother's cat yawning. Most alarming, my dear Whatmore. One would say, in atrocious pain. One wondered whether the jaw—"

"Well, there you are. I want you to look happy, agreeable, and comfortable. Look at yourself in the glass and sing loudly, you scowl most horribly at times. I want you merely to mouth the words, never mind the notes, and look pleasant. Try it in front of your glass."

"Franz will think I am quite demented at last. But what do you do about the voice? Do you, then, not require it?"

"Oh, we dub it later," said Whatmore. "You'll see."

"Oh," said the Graf doubtfully, "shall I? I want to say something about the scenes with the innkeeper's daughter. Would it be—"

"I heard from her, at last, this morning," said Whatmore, and the Graf stared at him. "She is Siegelinde Ohlssen, no doubt you've seen her. She's very good indeed, of course. And very expensive," added Whatmore, pulling a face. "I am going to take all her scenes together; I hope that a week of Fräulein Ohlssen will see us through."

"But—"

"I will take the rest of you through your parts in those scenes beforehand in order to save time. Perhaps Aurea would walk through the

Ohlssen's part for us; I wouldn't dare ask most actresses to do a thing like that, but she's very good-natured. A very nice girl indeed, Aurea."

"She is a very charming young lady indeed. What I have been trying for some minutes past to ask you is whether you would very kindly find someone else to take my part in the scenes with Ceci—with the innkeeper's daughter. Nothing has impressed me more," continued the Graf loudly and rapidly in order to forestall Whatmore's evident intention to refuse, "than the wonderful way you can cause things to appear to happen consecutively when in point of fact they were done upon entirely different days and in inverse order. I need only to particularize the occasion when I slid down a drainpipe to get away from an infuriated baker on Monday whereas he did not chase me across his bakery with his bread knife until Wednesday and I did not even meet his charming daughter until the following Saturday. What I was about to suggest, my dear Whatmore, if you will allow me, is that some man of my build with hair of my color and dressed in my clothes should actually play in those scenes, keeping his back to the camera and—"

"I never heard such infernal nonsense in the whole of my life," exploded Whatmore. "What the hell's the matter with you? I know you couldn't stand Beauregard but—"

"Beauregard's intentions toward the charming Fräulein Goldie were not such as could be tolerated," said the Graf firmly.

"Oh, weren't they? Then she had only to complain to me and—"

"And then he fell down the stairs."

"Yes. What are you laughing at? But why don't you like Fräulein Ohlssen? I suppose you've met her before too and had a row over—"

"I assure you with the utmost sincerity that I have never even had the pleasure of seeing the *gnädiges* Fräulein. Not only do I not know her, but I know nothing whatever about her. It is not personal at all. It is the scenes which—"

"Have we really," demanded the irritated Whatmore, "got to have all this trouble over the script again and again? I thought you'd got over that nonsense. I will take your advice with pleasure over minor points of manners and customs since I must say you seem to have that period at your fingertips, but when it comes to ridiculous and unworkable suggestions about the production I must tell you bluntly, Reisenfern, that I—"

"Please," said the Graf, "please. If it is to upset you like this I say no more. I am sorry, believe me, for suggesting it at all. My reasons concern no one but myself and are, I can see, of no importance whatever. I will play the scenes as you desire."

"Good," said Whatmore and, still snorting, he strode indignantly from the room. The Graf sighed.

"So," he said to Franz, "I have to play out in public a travesty of those moments which are among my most treasured memories. If my wife, the Gräfin Cecilie, knew what I—"

"She would laugh," said Franz.

"What?"

"The most excellent Gräfin would laugh herself into stitches," persisted Franz. "She was always laughing and a thing like this—" He spread his hands.

"Herrgott! I believe you are right. Franz, I am becoming ponderous and solemn. It is all wrong. If I let myself deteriorate like this she will not know me. She will not wish to know me and she will be quite right. Franz, what is the matter with me? I used not to be like this."

"It is all this work. My Herr has never worked before in all his life and now, for hours every day, he walks and stands and speaks as he is bid, sometimes over and over again till it would make the soul vomit to watch him. Work!" cried Franz passionately; "it is a curse laid upon us from our father Adam and his apple woman, it is no wonder that it should depress the spirits. Let the Herr rejoice, it will not be for long."

"But you, Franz, you work—"

"For my sins, doubtless," said Franz with his sudden wide grin. "Never mind, they were worth it."

"Franz!"

"If the Herr Graf will excuse me, there is an order to give about the wine." He left the room to speak to the majordomo; when he came back along the passage the sound of a cheerful voice lifted in song penetrated even through the solid door. Franz smiled to himself, opened the door and stood staring.

The Graf was standing, close in front of a mirror, with hands clasped over his heart, singing at full stretch of his lungs.

> *"In this cool cellar here I sit*
> *Upon this cask reclining—"*

He broke off and said: "Horrible, horrible. The Herr was quite right, I look like a baboon roaring."

"Please?" said Franz.

"Or like a dog baying the moon. You know, Franz, one sees other people looking awful but without ever realizing that one looks far worse oneself. Why didn't you tell me I looked like some of the worse gargoyles on Notre Dame?"

"In singing, a certain distortion of the distinguished features is inevit—"

"My most distinguished feature seems to be a large pink tongue. Wine, Franz. The pink"—he inspected it—"is turning brown. Quick, before I shrivel up." He drained the silver cup at a draught. "Now to take it more easily."

He arranged his pleasant features into an ingratiating smile and started again.

"In this cool cellar here I sit— Lieb' Gott, that's worse. I look like old Gustav at Heidelberg trying to borrow five marks. One does not smile too much. Once more. *In this cool cellar—"*

There came a knock at the door. Franz went to answer it and announced lunch.

"Perhaps after lunch," murmured the Graf, "song will rise to the lips more naturally."

The tavern set in the Bonn studio looked extremely well. Dark beams crossed the low ceiling and the lights of oil lamps against the walls were thrown back from polished brass and copper. Narrow heavy tables stood about; seats against the wall, benches and wooden stools awaited the company; over the great open fireplace were crossed guns and a stag's head borrowed from the castle of Grauhugel. The company strolled in; a dozen or so young men from the University of Bonn in property clothes and augmented whiskers disposed themselves about the tables in admirably carefree attitudes; among them was the young Graf von Grauhugel with Franz behind his chair. The company had been provided with some idle chatter to serve as background noises, the Graf and a couple of friends were about to discuss hunting, and Whatmore looked over the scene with an anxious eye.

"All right," he said. "Carry on."

"But," said one of the students, "where's the beer?"

"Just coming—here it is." Potmen in baize aprons bustled in with three or four steins in each hand, the appointed babble of talk began, the cameras started to whirr, and the Graf leaned across his table.

"Come down to my place in the vacation and we will find you a boar or two. When I was—"

There was a howl from some of the students. Whatmore signed to the cameraman to stop.

"What—"

"Beer?" said the students. "This isn't beer. It's water. Dreadful stuff.

Gets into your legs and gives you dropsy. We use it for washing. No beer, no song."

"But I never said—"

"No beer, no song."

The Graf disentangled himself from his circle and came to Whatmore.

"My dear fellow, this won't do. No, really."

"But the drinks in plays are never real! They're always—"

"I can't help that," said the Graf. "German students don't drink water. No German drinks water."

"But they will all get tight," said Whatmore.

"Oh, you need not to give them so much as all that! It would take far more than you think to do that. Two or three steins each is quite enough—more than enough."

"Two or three—what, three dozen or so?—I can't afford it," said Whatmore desperately. "I thought they understood!"

"Apologize, quickly, tell them a mistake has been made and shall at once be put right. I'll pay for it—quick! They are preparing to go! Franz, go across to the tavern opposite, run!"

Whatmore, scarlet with embarrassment, did as he was told, the students smoothed their knitted brows and sat down again, and the reinforcements arrived. The Graf resumed his conversation which naturally led up to a hunting song, followed by "O Tannenbaum," " 'Tis all one to me," and a reasonable expurgated version of "There were three travellers crossed the Rhine." This being one of those songs which go on and on, it was only natural that an argument should arise about how it did go on; one thing led to another as things do when there is plenty of beer about, and Whatmore successfully steered his scene to the point where the Graf became involved in a duel.

At this point the producer stopped the show, wiped his brow, and said that that would do for today, thank you.

The duel scene had been arranged with some care as was plainly necessary if no one was to be hurt. Whatmore had asked the actor Reisenfern if he could fence.

"I did a certain amount of fencing at one time," said the Graf. "Why?"

"Because there is a duel scene. I've got a man who really is an expert to be your opponent so that there won't be any accidents. He was at one time fencing instructor to one of the student corps here, the Borussia or some such name. All you have to do will be to stand up to him and at the end there will be a sudden breakoff and his cheek will be bleeding. Or appear to be, I don't intend you to damage him, naturally. If you know how to go through the motions, that's all that's wanted. He won't hurt you and he can defend himself."

"I think I can manage that."

"Of course, we shall have a rehearsal."

The rehearsal proved to be short. The fencing instructor was a man very sure of himself and with justice, since a man chosen to instruct the Borussian Corps must be brilliant indeed; he took one look at the Graf's slim form, amiable expression, and shining fair hair and said that if the young gentleman had the rudiments of the art and knew how to hold his weapon, how to salute properly, and also a few simple parries, the thing was as good as done. The Graf smiled, fencing foils were produced, and they exchanged a few passes.

"Not at all bad," said the instructor kindly. "If I had the Herr twice a week for a couple of years, he would turn out to be a very fair performer. Remember, please, to keep the wrist up."

"Thank you so much," smiled the Graf. "So kind of you."

That evening a pair of fencing foils were missing from a cupboard in the castle armory and at odd times in the next few days thuds and stamping noises could be heard in the Graf's apartment. The Graf had gone into training, murmuring of carte and tierce.

He lowered his point to the floor and thoughtfully massaged his right elbow.

"I made a mistake, Franz," he said. "I lacked foresight. I should have had you taught fencing. It would have been better practice for me than this *tirer au mur* at a palliasse with chalk marks on it."

For there was a hard straw mattress set up against the wall with the outline of a man chalked on it and divided into quarters according to the theory of fencing. It was a little reminiscent of the diagrams sometimes seen in butchers' shops to illustrate the division of the beast into joints.

"I thank the Herr Graf," said Franz stolidly, "but I think that I should be more useful unperforated, by permission."

His master laughed and went through the motions of a neat "double on both sides of the arm."

"It comes back," he said contentedly, "it comes back, though I don't know why I bother with that performance. That fellow would have half a dozen times thrust at me while I was going through all those disengagements."

"The man who told the Herr to keep his wrist up," growled Franz, for this is a maxim which has continually to be hammered into beginners.

"I thought it best," said the Graf mildly. "He may as well think me a child in these matters. Besides, it is not good form to show off."

"In the old days," said his servant, "it was the custom to lay bets in the course of a contest. If it is still done, have I the Herr's permission to take some of our money for the purpose?"

"Certainly, but I warn you, you may lose it."

"*Pfui,*" said Franz.

"Not *pfui* at all; this man is quite good and I am out of practice. Franz! Was that where some of your surprisingly large savings came from?"

"By permission, yes. When the Herr fought the original duel with the Baron von Hohenlinden which we are now reproducing, I more than doubled my wealth."

"The devil you did."

The duel took place in a beer garden kindly lent for the purpose by the tavern-keeper who had benefited by the earlier beer-shifting contest when the songs were sung. He had, to his delighted surprise, actually been paid in full. The beer garden was a pleasant spot with vines trained upon a trellis to form an openwork roof through which the sunbeams filtered. The tables and benches had been withdrawn to the sides, leaving a clear space in the middle; the students were disposed about this space and told to register an intelligent interest in what was going on, and three cameras at three points of vantage were trained upon the scene. Franz wandered round quietly between the tables, speaking to one and another.

"Now," said the instructor, "before we begin, let me remind the Herr that we are using rapiers today and not fencing foils with padded tips. Let not the Herr trouble his head about hurting me because he won't get a chance, but let him not crowd in on me or make any silly sudden rushes at me as he might possibly run himself upon my point before I can avoid him. Ordinary care, ordinary care, and all will be well. Understood?"

The Graf bowed, Whatmore looked a little anxious, and the scene was set. The two seconds, drawn sword in hand, led their principals forward and placed them; the duelists went through the grave and formal movements of the salute. Then—ah, they are at it!

The students, who knew very well how the alleged duel had been arranged, expected no more than some more or less adequate miming. Dueling has been forbidden in Germany for some years now—Hitler finally stopped it—but fencing is still a hobby and considered a graceful and healthy exercise. Most of the students there knew a good deal about it and some were fencers themselves. They began by looking on in a casual and patronizing manner, then their faces changed and their attention was riveted. Even Whatmore, who knew nothing about the art, realized that he was seeing something exceptional and signed to the cameras to carry on.

The rapiers clashed and slithered, an exciting sound which goes back through centuries of conflict. The pseudo Baron von Hohenlinden began with a confident air and a patronizing smile, but in a matter of moments his lips straightened and his brows came together. The dappled sunlight flashed from the steel as attack and defense, thrust, parry, and riposte came so rapidly that the eye could scarcely follow them.

The instructor was an older man, possibly stronger in the wrist and steadier; the Graf was lighter on his feet and astonishingly quick and accurate. The conflict was so even that the students forgot the cameras and the film and rose to their feet, almost forgetting to breathe.

Suddenly the Graf sprang forward, there was a double clash, a flash of sunlight as he lunged and his rapier point slid past his opponent's face, out and down and he stepped back. The seconds jumped in and crossed their swords between the combatants.

The instructor changed his sword from his right hand to his left, put his fingers up to his ear, brought them away and stared at the red upon them.

"Donnerwetter," he said, quite mildly, "the young devil has nicked me."

Chapter 9
PLATE ARMOR

WHATMORE AND DENMEAD, with other members of the company, including the Graf Adhemar and Aurea Goldie, watched the rushes of the duel scene the following day.

"Philip would not let me see this being shot," she said. "I do think it was mean of him. He said that if anything went wrong I would scream, as though I should!"

"I am sorry if you were disappointed, but in honesty I must uphold Denmead. A duel is no sight for a woman."

"But surely, when it is only acting!"

The Graf lifted his shoulders. "Indeed, the risk was not great, but they were real rapiers, you must know, and an accident might have happened. If one of us had slipped, for example."

"Then what?"

"Hospital for one, *gnä'* Fräulein! Wait till you see it for yourself."

The room darkened and the beer garden came up on the screen, the students leaned back against the walls or sprawled over the tables as the seconds led their men forward. The scene developed before them and ran its course until the film came to its end and a plain square of light showed on the screen.

"Pleased?" asked Denmead as someone switched on the lights.

"Pleased!" said Whatmore. "I tell you that scene will make the film when it's properly cut and edited. Bert! Run it back and put it through again, will you? One or two things I want to look at again."

"Philip was quite right," said Aurea. "It's just as well I was not there, I never saw anything so deadly. It makes me shake just to see it. How could you go through with it like that?"

"There was no danger," said the Graf. "We did not mean to hurt each other. Like other things, it is not so hard when you know how and have much practice."

The room darkened and the film started again.

"Look at that instructor fellow," said Whatmore. "Fine figure of a man and knows it. Look at the confident smile. He's just playing at it, you can see—now, look. See his face change? That's not acting, that's what he really felt like. 'Blimy, what have I got here?' See?"

"He's forgotten the camera," said Denmead, "and all I told him about not turning his back on it and keeping—look at that. You'd swear he was fighting for his life."

"Reisenfern is terribly good, I wonder where he learned to fence like that."

"Ask Franz. The instructor fellow said the same thing when I was mopping up his ear for him. He said it was absolutely first class but oddly old-fashioned. Then he went into technicalities so I brought on the iodine. I say, you're going to have some fun getting all those clashing and slithering noises absolutely in sync."

"It shall be done, though. Denmead, that's the main scene in this film, I don't know when I've seen anything so exciting. Look at those students, absolutely rapt. Ah, there's the end."

The lights came on again and Whatmore went to speak to the Graf.

"I am absolutely delighted, I do congratulate you. That was a wonderful show—" and so on, while Denmead strolled round to where Franz was waiting.

"Franz."

"Mein Herr?"

"What were you doing, strolling round at the beginning of that scene? I mean, it looked all right, but what was it all about?"

"Bets, mein Herr. With my Herr's permission, I laid a few here and there at good odds, they were so sure of their champion, you understand. Then, when they saw how the play went, they were not so sure and the odds shortened. Besides, I myself, watching, I forgot even about money. It was exciting, yes?"

"Very exciting. Franz, who taught your Herr to fence like that?"

"His highborn father, mein Herr, who was himself really first class. He had to be. When my Herr was quite a little boy, he had a little sword suitable for his size and so he learned and practiced all the movements, his father upon his knees to oppose him. A pretty sight, mein Herr."

"It must have been. Your Herr's father, was he an instructor, then?"

"Oh no," said Franz in a shocked voice. "Certainly not. Only of his own sons, for his own pleasure. Also, later, the boys used to fence together, but my Herr was always the best."

"I see. It was your saying that the Herr's father 'had to be good' that made me suppose—"

"Oh no. That was only in order to remain alive himself. He was a very lively gentleman, my Herr's father, and there were always the little difficulties occurring. The ladies, you know," said Franz confidentially.

Denmead's mind went back to an early argument about the script; Reisenfern, speaking as the Graf Adhemar, saying something about his father in Paris and one Cora Pearl.

"That kind of thing seems to run in the family," said Denmead.

Franz, in the act of turning away to follow his master, threw one of his sudden grins over his shoulder as he went.

At the head of the flying staircase, which went up from the entrance hall, there was an upper hall from which rooms and passages opened off, a bare, rather chilly space, unfurnished except for a few penitentially hard chairs against the walls and lit by a tall window at the far end. There were a few displays of weapons on the walls, otherwise the space was enlivened only by eight suits of armor of various dates which stood like statues at regular intervals. The two on either side of the head of the stair were good examples of the heaviest and most cumbersome period of plate armor, suits which only a strong man could bear upon him and he only if he were mounted upon a strong horse selected not for speed but for endurance in bearing burdens.

It must have been a wild and beautiful sight in the fifteenth and sixteenth centuries to see a knight being prepared for battle. He started off in shirt and breeches which were often made of chamois leather to prevent, if possible, chafing. Of course it was not possible to prevent chafing; the knight, as he tried to ease his person from the sharp edges which nibbled at him, could only say to himself that without his leather shirt he would be more uncomfortable still. Free and lissome in his light attire he stepped gaily across to where his squires awaited him and then the serious business of life began.

They proceeded to cover him completely with plates of metal shaped to fit approximately the rounded form beneath; with piece after piece they closed him in; breastplate, backplate, five pieces on each arm, six on each leg, a separate piece, the gorget, round his neck, and a helmet on his head. By this time the knight was so immobile as to be practically statuary and it is a fact that if the poor wretch fell on his back he could only wave his arms and legs feebly until someone came along and either helped him up or put a period to his misery with a dagger slipped in between the helmet and the gorget at the spot where even the most celebrated warrior keeps his jugular vein.

The knight, once completely encased, strode or tottered outside to where his horse, also armored over vital spots, awaited him, and clambered or was hoisted aboard. The knight had, of course, a sword at his left side and a dagger at his right; once upon his horse he was handed up a lance. In case he broke or dropped this, there was a mace hanging at his saddlebow with which to smite the ungodly. Someone put the reins into his left hand and slowly, but with immense dignity, horse and rider moved off. There was a hinged lid called a visor on the front of the helmet, but this was only closed at the moment of conflict since it was barely possible to see out of it.

In short, the mounted knight in armor was the tank of his day.

Franz was filling an idle moment by strolling about the passages from the upper hall when he encountered one of the housemaids. She was a pretty girl and he looked at her with obvious approval. She tossed her head and walked away, so he followed.

"Hey! Just a minute!"

"Certainly not," she said, and broke into a run. He ran after her, but she dodged into Aurea's room and stuck out her tongue at Franz as she disappeared. The next moment apologetic sentences floated out through the open door.

"Ach! *Gnädiges* Fräulein! I beg a thousand pardons! I did but come for the tray. I did not think the *gnädiges* Fräulein was here. Such manners—"

Franz walked quickly past the door into the upper hall and looked about him. If one of those suits of armor uttered a hollow groan or said "Boo!" as the maid passed—

Aurea came out of her room as Whatmore was coming along the passage and together they went toward the stairs. Her heels were tapping on the stone floor while Whatmore's crepe rubber soles made no sound, and until Aurea spoke at the head of the stair Franz thought it was the housemaid.

"Are you rehearsing those— What's the matter?"

Whatmore turned on the second stair and glanced back.

"This place is getting hold of me. I could have sworn I saw that suit of armor move."

"Nonsense," said Aurea. "What, that one in the corner? An optical illusion. What—"

"It made a noise," said Whatmore, staring. "A sort of creak."

"I expect it's getting rusty and it slipped or something. Do come on, you're making me nervous, and they're waiting for us."

They ran down the stairway together, but as they reached the bottom the sound of ponderous but unsteady steps above made them look back. The suit of armor was wavering upon the top step.

Aurea screamed. "It's coming after us!"

"Somebody playing a practical joke," said Whatmore, and even as he spoke the figure lost its balance, staggered, and fell headlong down the stairs with loud crashing noises and a howl of pain. It rolled down the last half of the stairway, disintegrating as it came, until it finished at the bottom in a heap of disconnected pieces.

"Some damned fool pushed it," said Whatmore angrily. Aurea was unashamedly clinging round his neck and he patted her shoulder. "Let go of me, there's a good girl, I want to run up and—"

People arrived, running, from all directions; Klaus, the majordomo, in a state of fuss; Denmead and the electrician called Harry and most of the company. At the head of the stairs appeared the housemaid.

"Here," said Whatmore, transferring Aurea to Denmead, "is there anybody up there?" He began to run up the stairs.

"No, mein Herr, please, only one of the armor figures has fallen, mein Herr, please."

"I noticed that myself," he said. "Is nobody about? Franz was there a moment ago."

"He went down, mein Herr—"

"I am here, mein Herr," said Franz, coming out from behind the stairs, "is there a need for something?"

Whatmore leaned over the balustrade and looked at Franz, who was limping and had a red swelling rising almost visibly upon his forehead.

"What's the matter with you, have you hurt yourself?"

"I fell over a chair, if it please the Herr, when I heard the noise, I was so startled."

Klaus and the electrician were picking up the pieces.

"These strap things," said Harry, "seem to have broken. I expect they're pretty old, aren't they?"

"But that wouldn't make it walk," said Aurea.

"There was somebody behind it walking it, m'dear," said Whatmore, "and if it's one of us there'll be trouble. I will not have this hooligan damage in a place that's been lent to me. Whoever did it ought to be damn well ashamed of himself. When I find out who's responsible he goes straight back to London! Now, which of you was it?"

"Dilly, dilly," said Denmead into Aurea's ear, "come and be killed."

But every member of the company seemed to have a quite unimpeachable alibi.

Some time later the Graf sat in his usual chair in his own suite with a glass of wine at his elbow and a cigar between his fingers.

"Franz. Leave off fussing with those clothes and come here."

Franz came and stood before the Graf like a schoolboy called up to the master's desk. He was no longer limping, but the bump upon his forehead approached its zenith.

"Mein Herr?"

"You will now tell me exactly how a valuable suit of armor came to roll down a long flight of stone stairs and seriously alarm a lady who is an honored guest in my house."

Franz wriggled.

"I saw Lieschen—" he began.

"If she's the black-eyed one with the coronet of curls I am sure you did. Go on."

"I spoke civilly to her and she put out her tongue at me and ran into the Fräulein Goldie's room. So I thought that if I were in one of those suits of armor and said 'Boo!' as she passed, she might be glad of someone to cling to. So I dematerialized and got inside and materialized again. But, Herr Graf, what a moment! It is so tight one cannot breathe and my feet were in agony in those iron shoes—"

"It is true that you have regrettably large feet."

"I heard the tap of high heels and assumed it to be Lieschen, one cannot see with the helmet shut—"

"The visor closed."

"The visor closed, but I thought I would endure till she had gone by. But when the lady came straight before me so that I could see, it was the Fräulein Goldie with the Herr Whatmore. Exactly then, I became aware that I was detached from the wall. I must be, by permission, a little taller than the highborn original owner, and my body lifting the upper part of the armor a little, unhooked it from its bracket. I began to sway and the Herr Whatmore noticed it. He said so, but the *gnädiges* Fräulein pulled him on and they went down the stairway. But, for me, I had begun to sway and could not stop; I could not move my arms. I was compelled to advance step by step as though I were in the grip of some diabolical machine—"

"You are making my flesh creep."

"I was irresistibly compelled toward the head of the stair; mein Herr, I swear I was guided that way—"

"By the ghost of the Graf Maximilian?"

"Please?"

"The highborn original owner."

"Very possibly. The next moment I was rolling down the stairs and before I could collect myself to dematerialize I got this"—Franz touched his forehead—"and other even more painful and undignified damage in less conspicuous places. *Herrgott,* how that armor does pinch! I regret, from the bottom of my heart, having alarmed so gracious and charming a lady, but I did not intend—"

"You *dummkopf,"* said the Graf, "why didn't you dematerialize when the armor came off its hook? It would have slipped down in a heap and no one would have thought anything of it."

"Herr Graf, I did not think of it in time."

"No. You have to stalk forward five or six paces like an elephant on parade, you—you—"

"Numbskull," suggested Franz humbly.

"Idiot," said the Graf.

"Blockhead," agreed Franz mournfully.

"Mooncalf!"

"Dunderpate."

"Clodpoll!"

"Jobbernowl," said Franz, squinting horribly.

"Get out!" said the Graf with a shout of laughter. "No, come here. Pour out a glass of wine for yourself, wine is good for bruises."

"I thank the Herr," said Franz. "By permission—"

"Well?"

"I am becoming quite expert upon my bicycle, I can now ride with one hand only holding on. If the Herr has any errands for me to do—"

"I will remember. In the meantime, you have my leave to continue practicing. Do not get into any avoidable trouble."

"Oh no, mein Herr," said Franz innocently. "Never."

Chapter 10
TWO HUNGRY MEN

THERE CAME a Saturday which was given to the film company for a day of rest, that is to say, a day upon which no work was done upon the film; but the sort of program which most of the company proposed for themselves would make a hard day in the studio seem in comparison like an afternoon in a hammock. It is very strange how high a proportion of the English cannot see a hill without instantly desiring to climb it, or a river without proposing to row upon it. In the Rhineland there is, naturally, the Rhine and there are also innumerable hills. The castle of Grauhugel emptied after breakfast and peace settled upon its corridors and terraces.

"What," asked Franz, pouring out the Graf's fourth cup of coffee, "does the Herr wish to do today?"

"I was kindly invited by the Herr Whatmore to drive in his car with him and the Fräulein Goldie and the Herr Denmead to Cologne, but I thought it wiser to decline. The police, you know. I am sure the Herr Whatmore would be most annoyed if the actor Reisenfern were arrested before his eyes and one cannot keep on vanishing every time one sees a policeman. Besides, to speak truth, Franz, I do not like vanishing suddenly. It makes me feel quivery and slightly damp. Taken slowly, it is not distressing."

Franz said that in his experience holding one's breath was a help at such moments.

The Graf said that he would try it at some appropriate time. "I thanked the Herr Whatmore for his kind offer but said that I proposed paying my respects to some old friends of my family whom I had not seen for many years."

"Is it the Herr's wish that I should procure some flowers?"

"Flowers? What for?"

"For the churchyard," said Franz, "naturally. One always takes flowers."

"Morbid idiot," said the Graf energetically, "I do not propose to spend a beautiful June day haunting churchyards. I was only making a civil excuse. The Herr Whatmore kindly asked if he could drop us anywhere, an expression which I take to mean 'convey us to.' I said that if he could conveniently drop us at Königswinter we should be greatly obliged, and we start at half past ten. Let us, Franz, like the three travellers in the song, cross the Rhine, shall we? I have a fancy to walk again along the river-bank by Rolandseck, as we used to do so many years ago. Eh?"

"It shall be as the Herr Graf pleases," said Franz happily. "I also remember with pleasure the further bank of the Rhine."

"Great-grandmothers," said the Graf, "every one."

Rolandseck must be one of the longest and narrowest villages upon the Rhine since it has to be squeezed in between the hills and the river. There is a footpath along the riverbank, divided from the road by a rough grassy strip; the Graf and his servant strolled along it in preference to the road.

"It is but little changed, Franz."

"No, indeed, mein Herr."

"Only in matters of transport," said the Graf, with his eyes on a fast motor launch going upstream at a pace which surprised him. "Motorcars, and such things. On the whole, a definite improvement. The common people, too, how well fed they look and how neat and tidy their clothing."

"They all wear shoes," said Franz, "even in fine weather."

"And the children also wear shoes, a strange thing which I never expected to see. The Rhineland must be very prosperous in these days."

"They say in the servants' hall that no one who is willing to work need lack employment. More than that, if a man dislikes his employment he can leave it and go to work at something else."

The Graf thought this over.

"Then who does the more disagreeable tasks?"

"The less intelligent, I suppose."

"I suppose so. Or, possibly, prisoners. These do seem to be happy days we have come back to, Franz."

A few yards from them two men were sitting on the grass, dividing, with careful accuracy, three cold potatoes between them. "Do not eat too fast, Erich," said one. "Make the good food last."

"I hope we get something more before tonight," said the other, "or we shall be hungry indeed."

They were men past middle age, clean and of respectable appearance; their clothes were well worn but cared for and had plainly been good once. The Graf stopped to gaze absently across the river and Franz, of course, stopped when he did.

"Did you hear that, Franz? They say that that is all they have to eat."

"Some misfortune must have befallen them."

They strolled on again; when they came level with the two men the Graf wished them good day and they answered readily and politely.

"A pleasant spot for a short rest," he said, and they agreed. "You are, perhaps, travelling?"

"We are looking for work, mein Herr."

"I hope you may soon find it. There does not appear to be much unemployment today, from what I hear."

"We hoped for work in some hotel, for that was our trade, but most hoteliers prefer younger men," said one of them. "Most of the hotels are already fully staffed for this season."

The Graf looked at them with interest.

"At your age, you were doubtless in good positions," he said, and they smiled.

"I, mein Herr, was the owner of a hotel," said the older of the two, "and this was my manager. That was in Silesia. We were too old for this war so we kept on with the hotel. Then the Russians came, but we still kept on. But now—"

"The Russians thought they could run it better than we," said the other with an angry laugh.

"They took over my hotel and told us to go away. So we went quickly, leaving all behind us. We did not wish to be sent to work in the mines."

"But this is disgraceful," said the Graf indignantly. "I know the Russians are uncouth and uncivilized, but surely they should pay you compensation."

The men stared.

"But, surely, the Herr knows—"

"But the Herr must have heard? The Russians do not pay, they take."

The Graf realized that he had run into unforeseen difficulties.

"I have had no personal experience," he said. "Scratch a Russian, they say, and you will find a Tartar. I am sorry for your troubles; I hope you will soon find better days."

The Graf and his servant walked on in silence for some time.

"I must be getting softhearted with the passage of years, Franz. I cannot get those men's faces out of my mind. That they should go hungry, in our Rhineland!"

"Should I go back, with some money for them?"

The Graf put his hand in his pocket and stopped in his tracks.

"Have you got any money, Franz?"

"Four or five marks—four marks seventy-five," said Franz, counting it. "I beg the Herr's pardon, I thought the Herr—"

"I left it on my dressing table. We have not enough with us to buy lunch for ourselves."

They looked at each other and walked on slowly until they came into a road of shops.

"By permission," said Franz, "I have an idea."

"Well?"

"If I were to dematerialize, I could transfer myself in a moment to the castle and bring the Herr his money from the dressing table."

"So you could. So you could. There is a shop there which sells food; let us go and look into the window."

The shop had sausages in great and surprising variety, some tinned goods, salads, and some meat pies. In the middle of the front of the window, as a *pièce de résistance,* a picnic basket, open to show its contents: a cold roast fowl, salad, rolls and butter, and a piece of cheese. Two bottles of wine leaned out of the basket and the lid was fitted with plates, knives and forks and two collapsible tumblers. There was even a little pot of salt. Propped up against the basket was a large white card inscribed: *Für den "picnic" 20 DM.*

The Graf cheered up at once. "That," he said, pointing it out, "is what we shall give them. Eh? We will have some fun with this, Franz. We will *both* dematerialize, and while you go for the money I will take the hamper to the poor men. While yet they sit there gazing with sad eyes into a hollow future, there will be a muffled thump and a hamper will suddenly appear before them. Then we can stand back and watch them eat, like good King Wenceslaus. We can pay for the food later. Excellent. Let us do so."

"For heaven's sake," said Franz, "let not the Herr Graf dematerialize here! The Herr is already beginning to thin out in full view of a bearded Herr of severe aspect who will certainly call the police—and here comes a policeman."

"There are also two small children and an elderly woman with a basket. You may be right, Franz, though indeed I cannot understand how the policeman could arrest men he cannot see. Let us retire into this alley for a moment. You know," continued the Graf, "it is a very odd thing that when we were here before no one ever desired to arrest us, not even in Paris, whereas now we spend our days dodging away from the police."

Their voices died away and the alley was empty.

The bearded gentleman of severe aspect walked heavily with a stick, for he was lame and elderly. He limped up to the window of the sausage shop and stood looking in; his cook had left him that morning and it was necessary to take home some cooked meat for lunch. Sausages? That cooked fowl looked very nice, but he had no use for the basket or the other contents. Presumably they would sell him the fowl separately. He stepped to the door and looked into the shop, but at the moment there was no one there. Probably upstairs on some errand. He turned back to the window, that fowl would do for two or even three meals—

It was not there. Neither the fowl nor the wine nor the rolls; basket and all were gone and in the vacant space they had occupied the white card lay flat. *Für den "picnic" 20 DM.*

He let out a howl of pained surprise and pointed an angry finger at the window. The children came running, the countrywoman waddled up, and the policeman strode across and saluted, for he knew the old gentleman well.

"Herr Zellerhoff! Is there—"

"Sorcery," said Herr Zellerhoff.

"Sorcery? What, witchcraft? What, magic? What—"

"All those things at once. Listen. There was a basket in that window with food in it, a fowl, cheese, wine—"

"*Ja, ja,*" said the countrywoman. "I myself, in passing, I saw it. A good fowl but not so fat as mine."

"Woman, be silent. The basket was there, in that space where the card is. Now—"

"Someone," said the policeman sensibly, "has been in the shop and bought it."

"Hold your tongue and listen. I looked at it, I took two paces to the left, so, and glanced inside the shop, there was no one there; I took one pace back, so, and looked again, and the basket was gone."

"The Frau Muller," began the policeman, referring to the shopkeeper.

"The Frau Muller," interrupted Zellerhoff, "was not in the shop. I said so just now. Cannot you understand plain German?"

"The Frau Muller," put in the countrywoman, "is, in fact, in the post office, I saw her but now. Here she comes."

"I can indeed understand plain German," said the policeman, "but I do not think that this is."

Frau Muller came bustling up, a thin anxious woman. "What is it, is there anything—"

"There is. There is your picnic hamper which has gone into thin air," said Zellerhoff. "Listen. I was looking—"

"My picnic hamper! Someone has stolen it!"

"No one stole it," said Zellerhoff. "I was here, I myself, and there was no one. Listen, I was looking—"

"Might it perhaps be," suggested the policeman, "that one in haste required your hamper and, not finding you in the shop, has left the money on the counter?"

Frau Muller dived into the shop and conducted a hasty but thorough search while the crowd at the window was augmented by a painter with a ladder, a young woman with twin babies in a push-chair, a postman, a river boatman, six more assorted children, and a nurse in uniform. The Frau came out of the shop again, wringing her hands, and saying: "No. It is not there. What a misfortune!"

"It is stolen, then," said the policeman, and engaged himself in thought.

"Since the war," said the countrywoman, "you can't trust nobody. Such queer characters there are about."

"It was not stolen," said Zellerhoff. "I was here and there was no one. I was looking at it. I took two paces to the left, so, and glanced—"

"The thief, carrying the basket, did not pass me," said the policeman. "Therefore he must have gone this other way. I go in pursuit." He turned from them and walked steadily away in the direction from which the Graf and Franz had come, glancing with professional keenness at everyone he passed, though one was the parish priest and another the policeman's own wife. The voice of Herr Zellerhoff, lifted on a tide of exasperation, floated after him.

"Listen. I took two paces to the left, so, and glanced inside the shop, there was no one there; I took one pace back, so, and looked again, and the basket was gone."

"What a misfortune! My so-expensive picnic basket—"

The two men on the riverbank had finished their cold potatoes. They lay back and closed their eyes, for the sun was warm and the grass soft; they had walked from Bad Godesberg that morning and men easily tire when they are half starved. Presently a voice spoke from somewhere just behind them.

"Meine Herren," it said, "luncheon is served."

"One has this kind of dream," said the elder man drowsily, "when one is hungry." He did not open his eyes, but his friend did and sat up with a start.

"Gott im Himmel, it is no dream! Look!"

The other also sat up, saw a picnic basket before him, with the lid thrown back to disclose unimaginable delights, and immediately looked round about him. There was not enough cover for fifty yards in any direction to hide a dachshund and there was not even a dachshund in sight.

"Who brought that—who spoke? Erich, did you see—"

"I saw no one. That basket—Rupprecht, is it real? I am almost afraid to touch it lest it vanish. They say that hungry men see visions and at least it is pleasant to look at."

Rupprecht considered. "Let us close our eyes while I count ten. Then, if it is still there, we will see if it is also palpable. One, two, three . . ."

At the word "ten" they reopened their eyes. A clean paper tablecloth was spread upon the grass and the fowl was upon it with the rolls, the butter, and the cheese. The salad was still in the basket with the wine bottles and the table utensils were still in their little loops on the basket lid. There is not much time, while a man counts ten, though Franz was quick and deft.

Erich stretched out a trembling finger and touched a roll, Rupprecht drew along breath and poked the fowl.

"They are real!"

"Now," said Rupprecht, "let all things be done decently and in order. Will you kindly lay the table, Erich, while I open one of these bottles? I still carry my corkscrew."

When all was ready they looked at each other.

"Now this is a miracle," said Rupprecht, the elder. "To whatever or whoever is responsible, in the name of God, thanks."

"Amen!"

When every edible scrap of the fowl had been eaten, when the rolls and butter and cheese had gone and the last leaf of the salad, when the first bottle was empty and the second had been broached, they leaned back on their elbows and laughed at each other.

"This," said Rupprecht, "is a glorious and wonderful day."

"A day never to be forgotten," agreed Erich.

"How warm and bright is the sun, how sweet the air."

"It only needs one thing to complete the picture—"

"Beware of greediness, Erich, we have been wonderfully blest already—what is it?"

"A couple of cigars, one each."

Rupprecht looked disapproving and then laughed. "You are right. These other things came while we had our eyes closed, did they not? Now, if we may, without being importunate—close your eyes, Erich, while I count twenty—"

"Twenty!"

They opened their eyes; there, upon the paper tablecloth, lay two cigars.

The policeman had walked at a good round pace right through the village of Rolandseck along the main road, with the railway close upon his left hand, past the bluff where stands the Arch of Roland, through Rolandswerth, and out upon the straight road to Mehlem. When he reached the outskirts he stopped.

"Carrying that basket," said the policeman, "he would not walk so fast as I. If he had a bicycle he is in Bad Godesberg by now. If Herr Zellerhoff is right, he does not exist. Why pursue a man who does not exist at six kilometers an hour along a dusty road upon such a hot day?"

The answer was so obvious that he turned round and walked back; when he came level with the motorboat landing stage he turned off the road and went down to the river. A short rest would be welcome. A smoke would be soothing to the nerves. He leaned upon a convenient rail and took a cigar out of his breast pocket, holding it between two fingers while he felt for his matches. When he got them out he had not got a cigar to light.

"I must be very tired," he said, "or sickening for some illness. I could have sworn I took out a cigar, but evidently I was wrong. I had two. I still have two, then." He put his fingers in his breast pocket. "Wrong again, I only have one. I will see to it that this one does not disappear like the other—"

But it did.

There was a motor launch going upstream between him and the island. The policeman looked fixedly at it, away for a moment, and then glanced back. The motor launch was still there.

"If I were one of those brilliant highly paid detectives they have in Bonn," mused the policeman, "I should ask myself whether there is any connection between the mysterious disappearance of a picnic hamper from Frau Muller's and the mysterious disappearance of two cigars from me.

There can be none. Oh, can't there? There is. There is me. I was there also."

He leaned heavily upon the rail.

"Am I suddenly afflicted with some power which makes things disappear? Kind heaven, please, no. One who makes things vanish cannot be a policeman. It would not be allowed."

He straightened his knees with an effort and walked on along the path by the river. A hundred yards further on he came upon two men lying in the grass. There was an empty picnic hamper at their feet, and they were each smoking a cigar exactly like his.

Chapter 11
THE FRENCH SALON

THE TWO EX-HOTELIERS upon the bank saw the policeman coming toward them with the evident intention of speaking to them. They greeted him cheerfully, for they had never had reason to be afraid of the police. The policeman himself was a little taken aback, for their greetings were friendly and not impertinent; moreover, they were plainly not common tramps and still less did they look like conscious thieves with the evidence of their guilt openly before them. As for Rupprecht and Erich, they were well fed, comforted with wine, and rested from their fatigue; the world was a nice place once more.

"You look hot and tired," said Rupprecht, almost forgetting that he was not in his hotel, "will you not spare a moment to rest yourself? It is very pleasant, sitting here."

"Thank you," said the policeman warily, but he sat down beside them.

"A little wine, perhaps?" said Erich. "One moment while I wash one of our tumblers."

He went to the riverbank and rinsed out one of the little tumblers in the Rhine while the policeman stared absently at the river. That motor launch had turned and was coming back, that at least had not yet vanished. He took the wine with a word of thanks, said "*Prosit,*" and drank some of it.

"You look troubled," said Rupprecht sympathetically.

"I am, perhaps, a little puzzled," admitted the policeman.

"Your duty," said Erich, "must often present itself in the form of puzzles to be solved."

The policeman sighed heavily and there was a short pause.

"At the moment," he said, "I am investigating the disappearance of a picnic hamper from the shop of Frau Muller in the village yonder. Just such a hamper as I now see before you, except that it was full and is now empty."

"Unlike us," said Erich, "who were empty and are now full."

"Precisely," said the policeman, and finished his wine. "It is my duty to ask you from where you got this one."

"Obviously," said Rupprecht. "You would be very remiss if you did not do so."

"Let me refill your cup," said Erich.

"Oh, thank you indeed—but I deprive you—"

"Not at all," said Rupprecht. "My friend and I can share the remaining—er—goblet between us. *Gesundheit!*"

"*Gesundheit!*"

"As for the hamper," continued Rupprecht, "it was given to us."

"I could not see you," said the policeman, "without being sure that you had some valid explanation. Forgive my uncivil adherence to the course of duty—who gave it to you?"

"As to that," said Rupprecht, "frankly, I do not know."

"A stranger, possibly," said the policeman, picturing the thief panicking at the thought of being caught with the basket in his hands. A sensible man would get rid of the evidence. "What was he like?"

"We did not see him," said Erich.

"Not see him? But—"

"We were asleep," said Rupprecht. "We had walked from Godesberg and were tired. When we woke, there it was."

"But," said the policeman sternly, "although you knew the food was not your property, you yet consumed it."

"Sir," said Rupprecht, "since it was given to us surely it was our property?"

"Let me refill your glass," said Erich, and poured out the last of the wine.

"Thank you, indeed. *Prosit!* But are we not arguing in advance of our knowledge? I will not conceal from you," said the policeman, "that it is not yet established that this is, in fact, the hamper which Frau Muller has lost. For me, all I can say is that it looks like it."

"The obvious solution to that," said Rupprecht, "is to go and ask her. Erich, will you kindly repack the basket?"

"You have relieved me," said the policeman, "of the painful necessity of asking you to come along."

"It is the part of a good citizen," said Rupprecht, rising stiffly to his feet, "to make the performance of a policeman's duty as little disagreeable as possible."

They went along together, like friends, after a polite squabble about who should carry the basket. The policeman won because, as he rightly said, it was evidence and he must take charge of it.

When they reached Frau Muller's shop there was still a group round the window, staring at the space which the hamper had originally filled. Herr Zellerhoff was still there and still telling his story to fresh comers as earlier group members faded away. The policeman, hamper in hand and closely followed by Erich and Rupprecht, strode up to the crowd. "Frau Muller! Inspect, please, this basket. Is it, in fact, the one which you lost?"

She came diving out of the shop door, a harassed woman, pushing back straying hairpins as she came.

"It is like it. How can I say? The food I might have identified, but that is gone. Who will pay me for it?"

"Who ate it?" asked Zellerhoff.

"We did," said the culprits with one voice.

"Tell me at once," said Zellerhoff, turning upon them, "how the devil did you get it out of that window? Eh?"

"We did not," said Rupprecht. "It was given to us."

"We have, in fact," said Erich, "never been in this village in our lives before."

"It seems," said the policeman judicially, "that that may very well be true. These gentlemen say that they were asleep on a grassy bank and, when they woke, there was this basket before them."

"But who will pay me?" asked Frau Muller.

"Where is this grassy bank?" asked a voice from the crowd. "If I go sit on it, do I get a jar of *Steinhager?*"

"More likely ants," said another voice.

"If you cannot identify the basket," began the policeman

"The point is unimportant," said another voice from the crowd, "since Frau Muller has now been paid. There is the twenty marks, in the window."

Everyone crowded round to look at two ten-mark notes tidily arranged fanwise on the price card. Frau Muller rushed back into the shop and seized the money.

"That is right! I am, indeed, paid. But how—"

"Then all is well," said Zellerhoff, "and you, Herr policeman, have no case. But as to how it was worked I have no idea."

"Erich ," said Rupprecht, and drew him aside. "That voice from the crowd—"

"Was the same," murmured Erich, "as the voice which said 'Luncheon is served.' "

"And the same as that gracious Herr's who spoke to us earlier."

The policeman walked heavily away. "What an afternoon! I lose my cigars and then I lose my case. I think I go home to bed." His hand went automatically to his breast pocket and checked suddenly, for there was something there. He pushed his fingers in and drew out two cigars.

"There is also something a little strange here," he said. "Mine were only twenty-pfennig cigars and these cost one mark twenty-five at least."

Herr Zellerhoff seized upon the ex-hoteliers. "Who are you and where do you come from?"

They told him.

"So now, mein Herr, we are looking for work."

"Indeed! What sort of work?"

"Household work of any kind. I owned a hotel and this was my manager when—"

"Can you cook? Can you keep house—"

Old Jakob, the castle clock, struck midnight in slow and solemn tones and Franz approached his master's chair.

"By permission—"

"What is it, Franz?"

"Mein Herr, it is now four—no, five—nights since you walked, if I may be excused."

"I suppose it is," said the Graf, putting down his book. "I left it for a few nights because I was annoyed by a boy who is servitor to the electrician, Harry. I met this boy in the north corridor on Tuesday night and he had the insolence to throw a book at me. It did not affect me in the least, of course, but I was seriously annoyed. What was he doing on that corridor? It would have served him right if I had kicked him down the stairs."

"As the Herr Graf did the Herr Beauregard."

Von Grauhugel laughed. "I seem to be making a habit of it. But the fellow Beauregard was annoying the Fräulein Goldie, a guest in my house."

"The boy is gone," said Franz, "he has been dismissed."

"Indeed? I am glad to hear it."

"Klaus came upon him prowling the corridors at night and complained to the Herr Denmead. The Herr had the boy brought before him, but when accused of looking for something to pilfer, the boy insisted that he was waiting to see the ghost again."

"Did anyone believe him?"

"I do not know, mein Herr. The Herr Denmead said that he could pack his things, catch the midday train, and look for ghosts at home. The Herr Denmead added that, until he had left the castle, he had better be careful not to fall downstairs."

"The Herr Denmead said that, did he? I have occasionally seen the Herr at night, but he made no sign. Am I altogether in the right form, Franz? All these different phases are a trifle confusing."

George Whatmore had heard a piece of news which greatly excited him. That internationally famous film magnate, Elmer Q. Axenstrasse, had come to Germany to visit one of his companies, which was making a film of Wagner's *Götterdämmerung,* of which numerous outside scenes were being shot in the authentic atmosphere of the Rhine. It was to be, of course, in CinemaScope in full color with a real Wagner orchestra, full choruses of men and maidens in costumes designed regardless of expense, the solos dubbed by operatic singers of international repute, and additional dialogue by Ken Polowski. Of the spectacular scenic effects it can only be said that it is a pity Wagner did not live to see them because he would have been enraptured with them beyond the seventh heaven of beatitude. "This," he would have said, "is what I really meant." The Valkyries swept from heaven to earth upon wide wings of thunder instead of sliding down chutes on rocking horses; the Rhine Maidens floated through a golden river flecked with pearl and opal. In a word, Elmer Q. Axenstrasse had got something there.

He also had a chain of cinemas throughout the United States of America and this was, to be frank, the reason for Whatmore's interest in him. It is well known that however successful a film may be in Britain it will never make a fortune for its promoters because the British market is not large enough, unlike the fantastic size of the cinema-going public in the United States. On the other hand, it is very difficult for a British film to receive a really wide showing in the United States because most of the cinemas there are under contract to take their films from Hollywood.

But, and this is where Whatmore's breath came short and his eyes were dazzled, if the great Axenstrasse took a fancy to Whatmore's unpretentious little film and casually consented to give it a showing in the Axenstrasse cinemas— At this point in his thoughts Whatmore always found that he had sprung from his chair and was striding agitatedly about the room.

Axenstrasse was staying in Bonn and making holiday in the intervals of encouraging his company; Whatmore, who knew some of them, had arranged to be introduced to the great man. With his knees knocking together with nervousness, he was shown into the magnate's suite expecting to meet a kind of amalgam of Mussolini, Primo Camera, and the Emperor Charlemagne; someone seven feet high and five feet wide, whose eyes shot lightnings and at the thunder of whose voice trees fell down flat.

In point of fact he met a rather small middle-aged man with a singularly quiet voice and a most friendly manner.

"Well now, Mr. Whatmore, they tell me we're both in the same game in this highly romantic scenery. Is that right—you're living in some wonderful old castle with armor in the hall and genuine family retainers on the stairs?"

After that everything seemed easy and Whatmore found himself inviting the American to dinner at the castle if he would care to come, telling him with careful understatement about the "funny little film" he was trying to make. "Of course, it would seem very small beer to you, sir. But it's rather fun, actually."

"The first film I ever made," said Axenstrasse, "was a terribly earnest thing about a lot of bad men chasing each other in cellars. A sort of chain of cellars opening one out of the other. I wouldn't know why, Mr. Whatmore, there simply had to be cellars but that's the way it was, maybe I had a fixation about it or whatever they call the darn thing. No, now I come to think of it, those cellars were symbolical, believe it or not, though what they were symbolical about has since escaped me. Whenever my wife— I have a very charming wife, Mr. Whatmore, who I am happy to say is joining me here next week—whenever Mrs. Axenstrasse thinks I'm getting a bit too—well, you know, a bit too satisfied with my career, shall we say, she threatens to take out this—this skeleton in my closet and stand over me while I sit through it. I have staved it off so far, but one never knows."

"I don't suppose for a moment that mine is anything earth-shaking, but I've had one stroke of luck. I've got an actor who really is something. I mean, he's so sunk in the part you'd think he really was the man he's playing."

"What's his name?"

"He calls himself Johann Reisenfern, but he admits that's not his real name, and if you try to ask him anything about himself he shuts up like a clam. I've left off asking, I might lose him if I annoyed him. There's no doubt he knows his period, all sorts of little details and exactly the right manner."

"Interesting. What is your period? Eighteen sixty-nine, eh?"

"If you really would honor me by dining with me at the castle one evening, I'd have him in too if you would care to meet him."

"That's most kind of you, Mr. Whatmore, and I'd be delighted to come. Let me call in my secretary and we'll fix up a date right now, if this week will suit you, because when Mrs. Axenstrasse comes I guess she'll have some plans ready for me. Well now—"

Axenstrasse came to dinner four nights later. He had signified his preference for a small stag party— "When Mrs. Axenstrasse is not with me I do not much frequent the company of ladies"—so the party was to be a small one, Whatmore, Denmead, the Graf, and the honored guest. Whatmore consulted the majordomo about the arrangements.

"A guest whom the Herr desires to honor by a small party apart from the others. Yes, yes. In 1912 when this house had the honor of entertaining the late Kaiser Wilhelm II of honored memory, the covers were laid in the French salon."

"The French salon—"

"The Herr has not seen it. If he would deign to follow me—"

Klaus opened a pair of folding doors in the paneling of the great banqueting hall. The film company had had their meals at a long table in the banqueting hall every day since they had come to the castle, but Whatmore had never noticed these doors before. This was not remarkable since they were of the same paneling as the rest, they made no break in the pattern, and the only signs of their presence were two inconspicuous door handles. Whatmore took two steps into the room, stopped and blinked.

"Pink satin and cupids," he told Aurea later. "Persuade old Klaus to show it to you. It simply isn't real."

"The Graf Stanislaus, father of the Graf Adhemar Hildebrand, brought these furnishings from Paris," said Klaus, pulling up blinds. "It is understood that he used it for small private parties."

The walls were paneled in pale pink silk embroidered with exquisite tiny wreaths of flowers, the Empire settee along one wall and the chairs were upholstered in pink and silver striped satin, the carpet was an Aubusson in pink and gray, and over the carved marble mantelpiece there hung a large picture by the elder Fragonard in his most melting mood. There were also cupids.

"Parties," said Whatmore thoughtfully.

"The curtains," said Klaus rather hastily, "are, of course, laid away, but they can quickly be rehung. They match the silk on the walls, if the Herr pleases."

"But are you quite sure we ought to use this room? I mean, it's so wonderful. It ought to be in a museum."

"It will do it good to be used," said the old majordomo. "Besides, the Graf would wish it."

Whatmore thanked him and went away wondering which Graf was meant, the tall saturnine Graf Sigmund studying metallurgy in London or the exceedingly lively Graf Stanislaus, who bought furniture in Paris in the 1850s.

"If such were his tastes," said Whatmore to Denmead, "I don't wonder he left his family a bit straitened in money. Who was it said so—oh yes. Reisenfern."

"Cora Pearl and all that," said Denmead.

"There's one thing; if that room doesn't rock Axenstrasse to the heels of his boots, nothing will."

The film magnate came in the agreeable mood of a man prepared to be pleased and was clearly delighted to be received as a guest in the sort of place which is more usually exhibited by a guide. The entrance hall enchanted him, the great flying staircase was, he said, just pure poetry, the picture gallery impressed him deeply and, incidentally, so did Klaus Förster, the majordomo. The banqueting hall was, said Axenstrasse, such stuff as dreams are made on——"Being a student of Shakespeare, believe it or not"—but when he was conducted into the French salon he struggled in vain for words and then fell silent.

"If you can't produce a film in this castle, young man," he said eventually, "you deserve to spend the next ninety-nine years turning out horse opera."

A moment later the Graf entered, very point-device in the evening dress of his student corps in Heidelberg, with his fair hair brushed till it shone like gold in the light of the silver cupid lamps, a monocle stuck in his right eye, and his servant at his heels.

"Mr. Axenstrasse, may I introduce Mr. Reisenfern, who plays the Graf Von Grauhugel in my film—Mr. Axenstrasse."

The Graf bowed from the hips, but the American seized him by the hand, shook it warmly, and then stood back and looked him up and down.

"My young friend Whatmore, here, told me that you played the part of a German baron so well that you practically were a German baron. Well, I see what he means."

The Graf, who had just heard himself being disrated at least two ranks in the social scale, since barons are fairly thick on the ground in Germany, merely smiled and said: "So kind of you," in his best English.

"But surely, I've seen your face somewhere before."

"My poor face," murmured the Graf, "it was never my fortune."

"I have it! In your splendid picture gallery I was privileged to visit just now, there was one which was the image of you. I take it, sir, you are some relation of the family here?"

There was a sudden hush.

"If I am," said the Graf in his careful slow English, "it is very far gone. In families, the old faces," he smiled, "they pop up again, yes?"

The majordomo struck the floor three times with his staff of office and announced that dinner was served; the American, who appeared startled, was guided to a seat and the soup was served.

"I am so stupid," said Axenstrasse, "I cannot speak or understand a word of German except 'please' and 'thank you.' You must please excuse me," he added to the Graf; "I have had to work so hard all my life that I just haven't gotten around to learning as much as I'd like."

"Oh, please," said the Graf.

Denmead asked how work was progressing on *The Twilight of the Gods* and thereby let loose a flood of technical discussion. Whatmore, still a little anxious about the success of his party, noticed that for the first time the majordomo was remaining in the room to oversee the service. What a good old boy he was to take the trouble; anyone would think that he knew how important this dinner was. He must be suitably thanked for his services. Whatmore was idly wondering whether to give him a tip tomorrow morning and, if so, how much, or whether to wait until the end of their stay, when he noticed something else. From the majordomo's point of view, the guest of honor was plainly not Elmer Q. Axenstrasse but the actor Reisenfern. Franz stood behind his master's chair throughout the meal; when a fresh course came in the footman handed it first to Franz who held it while Klaus served Reisenfern and only after that were the other diners served.

At this point Whatmore remembered suddenly that this was the first time that Reisenfern had eaten in company, his meals were always taken up to his room.

However, Axenstrasse appeared to notice nothing or, if he did, he may have thought that foreign customs differed from his own; in any case he seemed to be enjoying himself. He could hardly take his eyes from the decoration of the room and asked Reisenfern if he thought the family would mind a few notes being taken.

"Someday," said Axenstrasse, "a period room like this one will be wanted, and there'll be guys running around with picture books out of libraries, and artists sitting in museums drawing chairs and tables for the props office, and experts arguing their heads off about did sofas have two ends or only one, and I shall say, 'Hush, gentlemen, and I'll tell you. I know, because I've seen it with these eyes: They won't believe me but what the heck. But I do not wish to intrude in any way, Mr. Reisenfern, and if you tell me that I shouldn't take such an advantage of a visit to a private house, what you say goes."

"Please?" said the Graf, and looked at Whatmore, who translated.

"Ah," said the Graf, "thank you." He screwed his monocle more firmly into his eye and beamed upon Axenstrasse. "For what I know, it is all right. You notice what you like and write down, yes, please. But you understand, all this," he waved his hand round the room, "it is not German at all. It is French. Most French. My—that is, the von Grauhugel who make this room, he was in Paris very happy. He bring all this home to remember—to remind him of Paris. Understood? He was"—the Graf smiled widely— "a gay lad. I have it right?"

"This film you're making," said Axenstrasse to Whatmore, "is it about that gay lad? By the way, if you haven't settled the title yet, there you have one that'll take some beating."

"Gosh, yes! I'll keep that one in mind, though actually the hero of the film is not that man but his son. He was also a person of cheerful character and has this advantage, that his life story does not require so much— er—editing as his father's appears to need."

"That may perhaps be," said the Graf, "because his son drown when he was two-and-twenty only."

"You think if he had lasted a bit longer he might have shown his dad where he got off?"

The Graf looked blank until Whatmore once more came to his rescue.

"Ah, now I understand, thank you. There was between these men one great difference. The son was happily married to a wife he love very much; the father's wife was—how shall I put it—the daughter of a great house, greater than this von Grauhugel. She was a Wittelsbach, you know? Of Bavaria, yes. It was—" The Graf paused to arrange his words. "It was so very kind of a Wittelsbach to marry a von Grauhugel. Always she remember how kind it was of her. You understand? She was of very strong nature, I remember—I remember hearing stories when I was young. She do it all, you know? Yes. So the Graf Stanislaus, he to Paris went. Understood?"

"Perfectly. Oh, perfectly. Oh boy, and do I sympathize! Not that the present Mrs. Axenstrasse is in the least like that; I am a very lucky man indeed, much luckier than I deserve. She is a very sweet and lovely woman, the present Mrs. Axenstrasse. But when I look back—never mind that now." The American emptied his glass, which Klaus promptly refilled. "Tell me, Mr. Reisenfern, when you finish this film have you any plans?"

"Please? Plans for what?"

"For your future career. Mr. Whatmore, I hope before I leave tonight I may be allowed to see some of your rushes, if you will not consider the request an intrusion."

"Delighted," stammered Whatmore, keeping his seat with difficulty since he wanted to jump up and down and cheer, "delighted and honored. There is, actually, a duel sequence on which I should value your comments, though it isn't edited or anything yet. If you wouldn't mind."

"Mr. Whatmore, you don't have to edit rushes for me to see if there's anything there, believe me. Mr. Reisenfern, was he on in this sequence?"

"He was one of the duelists."

"Oh yes? And what did you fight with, Mr. Reisenfern? Pistols?"

"Rapiers," said the Graf with a deprecating look, "only rapiers."

"Only rapiers! But, Mr. Reisenfern, that's miles ahead of pistols as a spectacle. Swordfights every time, for me; only it's so hard you wouldn't believe it, getting men to fight with swords. They figure it isn't too safe, and they're so careful a child could see it's phony."

"Oh no," said the Graf with the confidence of the expert. "With the sword, one defends oneself, with the pistol, no. You cannot push aside a bullet."

Mr. Axenstrasse stared and murmured "bullet." Klaus and his footmen came round the table, clearing it for coffee, cigars, and brandy and the diners sat back in their chairs. Conversation was interrupted for the moment, only the gentle voice of Elmer Q. Axenstrasse could be heard at intervals, murmuring: "Bullet. Bullet?"

Chapter 12
ELMER Q. AXENSTRASSE

"SEEMS TO ME, Mr. Whatmore," said Axenstrasse, "that acting in one of your films should be listed as one of the Dangerous Trades. We wouldn't use bullets in acting, Mr. Reisenfern, only blanks. Good actors are scarce."

"Of course, of course," said the Graf. "That I realize. I was then to the true duel referring. No doubt, in a play, you make use of many most clever"—he hesitated for a word—"tricks?"

"Sure we do. Yes, sir, the film companies have got tricks to make things look like what they aren't that would make a medieval monk cross himself and call on the saints. Talking about tricks, have you seen this one?"

For the Graf Adhemar had inadvertently introduced the one subject which most delighted the simple heart of their visitor. He made a hobby of sleight of hand and had practiced it until he was really good; his long slim fingers and supple wrists had a power over coins and other small objects which was nearly occult, and the Graf was fascinated.

"When I was in Paris," he said, "there was there a man with playing cards in hand. Mein Herr, he took them one by one from the air. From my ear also. *Uberraschend! Erstaunlich!* Truly."

"I can do one or two simple tricks with cards," said Denmead, "but I am not in your class at all. Definitely not."

The Graf, who had had a little more wine than was his custom, was fired by emulation and had a brilliant idea.

"If you will excuse me for just a moment," he said to Whatmore, "I think I can show our guest something." He left the room accompanied, as always, by Franz. Outside in the banqueting hall, still brightly lit but empty, they had a short conference and the Graf returned to the French salon alone.

"Will you ask our guest," he said to Whatmore, "if he has ever heard of levitation?"

"Levitation," said Axenstrasse. "Things, and people, floating in the air? Why, sure I've heard of it, but I don't believe it. That's the kind of nonsense they try to put over at these séances." His face darkened. "Damned nonsense, if you ask me. All done with wires."

"So?" said the Graf who, as he had told Whatmore, could understand English better than he could speak it. "There are not any little wires here. No."

There was a marble clock upon the mantelpiece, a substantial object carved and gilded; the sides were brought out in graceful curves to carry the reclining forms of young women dressed principally in a coating of gold leaf. The Graf lifted it down and its weight made him grunt.

"Feel," he said, handing it to Axenstrasse. "No feather, I think. You agree, yes?"

"Darn thing weighs fifty pounds," exaggerated Axenstrasse, and handed it back. "Beautiful thing, though."

"You," said the Graf, giving it to Whatmore. "You agree, no?"

"I do," said Whatmore nervously, "but what are you going to do? I mean, for heaven's sake don't drop it"

"I will not, I promise. Denmead, you too."

"Very solid," said Denmead.

"Good. Now look."

The Graf turned toward an unoccupied space in the room, went through the motions of putting the clock carefully upon an invisible shelf, and took his hands away. The clock merely stayed where it was, in midair.

The company gasped, as well they might.

"Well, I'll be gosh-darned—I mean—"

"Oh, hang it," said Denmead, "that's impossible."

"For goodness' sake," gasped Whatmore; then, changing into German, "Reisenfern, be so good as to put that clock back on the mantelpiece at once. No, I mean it, please. The Graf Sigmund was good enough to lend me this place and I am responsible for the contents."

"Certainly," said the Graf amiably, and put the clock back where it belonged. "I did not wish to alarm. A pretty trick, yes?" He looked at Axenstrasse and noticed that he had lost color. The Graf walked quickly round the table to refill his guest's brandy glass and put it gently into his hand.

"Drink up, sir, drink up. I am sorry to have startled you so. Indeed, it is but a trick, quite simple when you know how." He went back to his chair and Franz reentered the room to stand behind it.

Axenstrasse drank his brandy and the color came back into his face.

"Well, I'll be the first to admit I never was so startled in all my life, no, sir, never. When I saw you let go of that clock I braced myself for a horrible crash, and when it didn't fall—well! Tell me, Mr. Reisenfern, how the devil did you do it?"

But Mr. Reisenfern only laughed and shook his head.

"There's the Indian rope trick," said Whatmore; "we've all heard about that but I never met anyone who'd actually seen it."

"There's the mango tree trick," said Denmead. "I saw that myself when I was out East. Of course it doesn't really happen, you just think you see it grow."

"Hypnotism, I suppose," said Axenstrasse. "I have a profound distrust, gentlemen, of hypnotists, spiritualists, mediums, séance-mongers and all their tribe. Mr. Reisenfern, sir, I was not alluding for a single moment to your very remarkable performance just now; nothing could be further from my thoughts and I regard it as a high privilege to have been allowed to witness it. No, I refer to those double-crossing fakes who pretend to supernatural powers in order to rake money out of anyone who is credulous enough to believe in them." He scowled blackly at his empty brandy glass; the Graf just lifted one finger an inch and Franz slid round the table to refill the glass.

"The point being," said Denmead, "that they only do it to extort money and not to help or console or even, like our friend here, to startle and amuse."

"Oh," said the American to Franz, "oh, thank you. This must really be my last or I shall see four duels at once in your film, Mr. Whatmore. Yes, Mr. Denmead, that's certainly so. They are men on the make and not, in my opinion, honestly."

"You speak," said Whatmore, "as though you have had some personal experience of these gentry." He looked across at Denmead, who nodded, finished his brandy, and left the room.

Axenstrasse sighed. "There is here," he said, "a fellow calling himself Professor Xavier. He runs séances for people to go to, to get messages from their dear departed. I could almost swallow that if the departed came and gave their messages direct, but will somebody please tell me why they have to talk through Big Chief Thick-Ear, the chief of the Jim-Jam tribe, or the Emperor Julius Caesar or a slave girl at the court of Belshazzar? Another thing. Why do the various dear departeds, who were mostly sensible down-to-earth people when they were alive, have to talk such brainless bilge now they're dead? Tell me that."

No one felt qualified to do so and after a moment poor Axenstrasse continued to unburden his breast.

"My wife—now, in most matters I have the highest respect for Mrs. Axenstrasse's judgment and good sense. I would as soon take Mrs. Axenstrasse's advice as that of most men I know, but she's been bitten with this bug. Why, just before I came away she told me my grandfather, Amos Axenstrasse, had given her a message for me which said that I ought to concentrate more upon spreading sweetness and love among my employees and not so much upon overseeing their work. I ought, he said, to gather them together upon the set every morning and start work with a nice rousing hymn like 'Shall We Gather at the River.' I mean—it's all very well to laugh, Mr. Whatmore, but if you knew my grandfather you'd laugh louder still and I told her so. Tommyrot. He was a hard-drinking, hard-swearing, hard-living old reprobate who wouldn't recognize a hymn if someone poured it out of a jug. No, no more, young man, thank you, I guess I've had plenty already. If my grandfather had had the sense to tell me where he'd put the title deeds of that Hollywood property he bought in 1902 I'd have listened to him. Well, my wife has a great friend who's been over here some time, she's the wife of one of our American generals over here, and she's crazy for Professor Xavier's séances. So my wife writes and says how she's looking forward to consulting this boob and she knows I won't mind because I know how it strengthens and consoles her. Mrs. Axenstrasse, gentlemen, is, thank God, one of the healthiest and soundest women I've ever met; she has had, again thank God, a singularly untroubled life and I spend my days making her happy and not, if I may say so, without success. Could I, do you think, have another cup of nice, strong, black coffee? If it's no trouble—" Franz poured it out. "So what I want somebody to tell me is, what does she want strengthening and consoling for? Eh?"

"Would it not be possible," suggested Whatmore, "to have this phony professor chased out of Bonn? I mean, I should think his influence—"

"He has been," said Axenstrasse sadly. "He's in Königswinter now. You go by tram. Or river steamer." He sighed heavily and drank his coffee, which seemed to revive him. "That is, if you don't go by car. My car, but I have a strong feeling it will be otherwise engaged."

"It does seem," said Whatmore, "as though something ought to be done about this fellow." Denmead came back into the room and nodded to Whatmore, who went on: "If you really mean it when you say you'd like to see some of the rushes, everything is all set."

"Delighted, my dear boy, delighted," said Axenstrasse, springing to his feet with astonishing agility considering what he had had to drink. "I am looking forward to it with great pleasure. Shall we gather at the river, as you might say? Please lead the way."

When the show was over and Axenstrasse, declining further hospitality, had been affectionately seen off at the foot of the castle steps, Whatmore, Denmead, and the Graf Adhemar came back into the entrance hall together. Whatmore, abandoning the iron grip over his emotions which he had maintained throughout the evening, uttered a wild whoop of joy.

"He's taking it—he's taking it—he's going to take it. If the rest of it is as good as the rushes he'll take it for his chain of cinemas. Denmead, you heard him say it, didn't you?"

Denmead agreed.

"And I don't believe it was because he was a bit woozled, I think he really did like it. Don't you, Reisenfern?"

"Yes, indeed," said the Graf. "I do think so. I see that this has make you very happy and I am so glad."

"And he says I can go over to Bonn and use any of his gubbins I happen to want. He gave me a lot of tips, too. Awfully nice fellow, don't you think? Thoroughly good scout. I only wish there was something we could do for him in return."

"Perhaps there is," said the Graf.

"Oh? What had you in mind?"

"Some opportunity might arise."

"If it does, we'll all grab it. I say, Reisenfern, you did realize, didn't you, that he was practically offering you a job too? In some film about the American Civil War; he said the period would be about right for you. Oh, of course, and you said you had read accounts of it in the newspapers. What did you mean by that?"

"My English," smiled the Graf apologetically. "It is so bad it is quite misleading. I only meant I had read accounts of it taken from contemporary documents."

"Of course, of course. No, I think your English is jolly good, really. It was your duel scene that really shook him. But fancy being offered a part in one of the Axenstrasse productions. You do realize, don't you, Reisenfern, that if he takes you on your fortune's made? At least, if you keep it up."

"If I keep it up," echoed the Graf. "Yes, it was most kind of him and I was deeply gratified. Most surprising. I will wish you good night, gentlemen. We shall meet again in the morning. I hope you sleep well."

He went, with his light step and easy stride, up the great staircase and turned toward his own apartments while the Englishmen stood in the hall looking after him.

"That's a queer fish, Denmead."

"I like him," said Denmead sturdily.

"Oh, so do I. It isn't that, it's just that there's something odd about him. For one thing, nothing seems to impress him much, have you noticed? This offer of Axenstrasse's would have sent most film actors off their heads with excitement. Not Reisenfern, he'd express the same graceful thanks if you offered him a new brand of cigar. Nothing excites him; you'd think he'd got a mind above this world's affairs. And, Denmead, how the devil did he work that trick with the clock?"

"I have not the remotest, most tenuous beginnings of an idea, but I'm glad I saw it. Come up to bed; it's past one in the morning and we start work at eight."

"It isn't only that, with Reisenfern, I mean. What he doesn't know about that period isn't worth knowing. Were you there when the props man got into a tangle over harnessing the horses to that carriage we un-earthed in the stables? He'd got the harness all laid out and a picture to help him, but he hadn't a clue which strap buckled up to which or how they went round the horses. Reisenfern laughed himself silly and then sorted it all out without hesitation. Reisenfern knows exactly what all the different servants have to do, how they do it, what they're called, and how they ought to behave. Yet, when he came in when I was telephoning the other day, he was absolutely taken aback. He hadn't an idea what I was doing. He called our typewriter 'that printing machine' and he wanted to open Aurea's camera to see how it took pictures. I mean, you'd think he'd been born again or something."

"Perhaps he has," said Denmead soothingly. "Come—"

"Re-something. Reincarnation, that's the word I was groping for. Do you believe in reincarnation?"

"I'll tell you at eight tomorrow morning," said Denmead. "Come on up to bed. You'll be half dead in the morning."

In the Graf's suite, Franz was waiting on his master while he undressed.

"That business with the clock went off very well, Franz. Poor Herr Axenstrasse was so startled I thought he was going to faint."

"By permission—"

"What is it?"

"If the Herr Graf desires me to hold some article in that way again, it would perhaps be better to choose something lighter. One is not so strong, dematerialized, as one is in human form and it took all my strength——I could not have held it much longer."

"Ah yes, I did not think. I had noticed that myself, when dematerialized. Next time it shall be something light, if there is a next time. Franz, I think we should do something about this Professor Xavier, who pretends to raise the dead. It is not dignified."

"It might be worse," ventured Franz.

"How?"

"He might actually do so."

The Graf looked at his servant.

"If he raised the noble spirit of your *hochwohlgeboren* father," continued Franz cautiously.

"That would at least enliven the proceedings."

"Or of your queenly mother—"

"Heaven forbid! But, Franz, I am serious about this."

"Certainly, Herr Graf."

"It would be easy for us to make hay of one of his séances, but I think something more is wanted. The man should be publicly discredited. If we knew something about his past—but I do not."

"By permission, I think the police do," said Franz.

"Oh, do they? Go on."

"There was talk in the servants' hall about fortune-telling, one story and another. Then one said that it would be better to go to the famous Herr Professor Xavier just come to Königswinter, he was said to be wonderfully good, and another said that was not possible, he charged too much, he was only for the rich. Then the head housemaid came down on the girls who were talking—she is a terrifying person, the head housemaid— and said that they should do nothing of the sort if it only cost fifty pfennigs, for he was a bad man. She has a nephew in the police, did the Herr know? No, indeed, why should he? The head housemaid said that her nephew told her that the police knew a lot about the Herr Professor but not enough to do anything to him. They were just waiting for the Herr Professor to slip up and then, the head housemaid's nephew said, they would pounce. If the Graf pleases, it seems it must be true since he was run out of Bonn, as I understood the Herr Axenstrasse to say at table tonight, and the head housemaid said so, too."

"So there is something against him."

"Yes, mein Herr. The Superintendent of Police here has been away in Bonn for three days attending a conference of high police officials on reorganization, if it please the Herr, but he is back now."

"I see. You may put out the light now, I am going to sleep, it is too late to walk tonight. Good night, Franz."

Chapter 13
THE INNKEEPER'S DAUGHTER

THE POLICE STATION at Königswinter is a corner house on the river front, a Victorian-looking house with bow windows and steps up to the front door. To this door there came, a few mornings after the Axenstrasse visit, the Graf and his servant. The Graf looked older than his years, for his hair was turning gray on the temples; he and Franz had learned something of makeup in the last few weeks. He wore a serious and preoccupied expression and an air of authority which sat naturally upon him; Franz, very stiff and formal, walked half a pace behind and, when he stopped, stood at attention. He was carrying a briefcase. The Graf stalked into the charge-room and stared so haughtily at the Sergeant on duty that he automatically rose to his feet and saluted.

The Graf sketched an acknowledgment and said: "Superintendent Muller in the building?"

"Yes, mein Herr, in his office." The Sergeant turned toward a further door and added: "Whom shall I announce, if you please?"

The Graf shook his head slightly. "Your Superintendent knows me," he said. "We met last week."

The Sergeant jumped to the conclusion which he was intended to reach, that this was one of the high police officials who had been at last week's conference at Bonn, and showed them into the Superintendent's office. The Graf strode in and shook the Superintendent warmly by the hand.

"Good morning, Superintendent Muller. You remember me, we met at Bonn last week. I come from Mainz," he added in reply to a slightly baffled expression.

The Superintendent's face cleared. "Of course," he said. "I beg your pardon, but the gathering was a large one and I do not think that we spoke together."

"I believe not," said the Graf casually, "though I remember seeing you there. Interesting meeting, on the whole. Well now, I called in to ask if you would be so good as to give me any information you may have about that fortune-teller who calls himself Professor Xavier. He lives here in Königswinter, does he not? I assume that you have his dossier."

For Franz had spent a couple of evenings entertaining the village constable and learning about police procedure. Franz had said that if, as seemed possible, his master went off to America—

The constable nodded. "It is understood in the village that your Herr was offered a princely post by the rich *Amerikaner* who was dining at the castle two nights ago."

"Exactly," said Franz. "I do not wish to travel so far. I have my reasons. I prefer to stay in my own country and I had thought about joining the police. Now, tell me—"

All of which information was conveyed to the Graf and enabled him to speak confidently and correctly about such things as dossiers.

"Certainly," said the Superintendent. "It was sent to me from Bonn when he was told to go from there and decided to come here. For me, I could have spared him."

"You may not have him much longer," said the Graf. "There was some idea that he was thinking of coming to Mainz and there were one or two stories about him. We wondered whether anything you had would—er—tie up."

(Franz had impressed upon his master that the police spent their days and nights making things tie up.)

The Superintendent unlocked a cupboard and took out a loose-leaf file.

"I am sorry," he apologized, "I am not authorized to hand this over—"

"No, no," said the Graf. "Just a general outline."

The Superintendent turned over pages and read out several items which, it was reasonably certain, Professor Xavier would much prefer not to have publicly proclaimed; the Graf nodded, grunted, took notes, and occasionally smiled.

"In all these cases," said the Superintendent, "we are reasonably sure but the proof is lacking. He would wriggle out of it. That suicide case at Düsseldorf for one. Again, he is suspected of black market dealings in currency—"

The Graf winced, but fortunately the Superintendent was not looking at him.

"—but all we know is that he was in with that gang. Well, mein Herr, I think that is all."

The Graf rose and Franz, who had been standing with his hands clasped lightly behind him, came smartly to attention.

"Most helpful," said the Graf. "Thank you. I was sure I should not apply to you in vain. I cannot go into details at this stage, but one of those stories, of which I spoke, came from Düsseldorf. Thank you. Good afternoon."

Franz opened the door and the Graf made his first mistake. When the Superintendent saluted he merely nodded kindly and walked out with Franz after him.

"From Düsseldorf," repeated the Superintendent, staring at the closing door. "What does that remind me—from Düsseldorf? I don't believe I saw that man at Bonn." Voices in the charge-room outside and retreating footsteps. "The representative from—*du lieber Gott!* Those are the two the police want in Cologne—" He was out of his chair and across the room to fling the door open. "Stop those two! Call them back! Hi!"

The visitors' heads were still visible turning the corner into the side road that goes up from the riverside, but they did not stop, they passed from sight. The duty Sergeant galloped down the steps, swung round the gatepost, and stopped dead.

"They have disappeared," he said blankly. "There is no one in the street. Have they, then, left something behind?"

"No," said the Superintendent, also staring up the empty street. "Those two answer the description circulated by the Cologne police of the two who escaped from the cells there along with a black marketeer. I knew I ought to know them. They said they came from Düsseldorf."

A couple of days later the German actress came, Siegelinde Ohlssen, a tall dark girl to make the perfect foil for Aurea's blond beauty. Siegelinde Ohlssen was a singer as well as an actress since she had to take the part of the innkeeper's daughter of Heidelberg who was the romance of the young Graf Adhemar's life when he was a student there. The actor Reisenfern was introduced to her, he bowed and kissed her hand, and she looked him straight in the face.

"I have been studying the script very carefully," she said. "You make the love and I fall in it, eh?"

"That is so, *gnä'* Fräulein."

"You are the nobleman and I the untutored maiden who is dazzled by your charm of manner."

"No, Fräulein, you have it wrong, it is I who am dazzled by your beauty and your charm."

"I am not in the least influenced by your wealth and position?"

"*Gott im Himmel,* no!" said the Graf violently. "Never that."

The girl raised her eyebrows. "I only wanted to make sure of my reading of the character."

"My rank is a disadvantage," said the Graf. "You would be much happier if I were a local official or a farmer's son."

"I am, in short, a sensible young woman at heart."

"Not at heart," corrected the Graf. "In every other way, yes."

"But I do my best to hide my feelings."

"Certainly. You are dazzlingly—that word recurs when I think of you—dazzlingly cheerful when I am present. It is only when I am gone that you lean from your window and sing 'Love in silence, nought revealing—' "

"Without looking to see if you are hiding behind the trellised vine!"

Whatmore, who was within earshot, moved away to speak to Denmead.

"This ought to go well," he said. "They're getting on like a house afire."

"Look well together, too, don't they?" said Denmead. "Yes, this bit ought to be all right."

But it was not. The scenes had been well rehearsed beforehand with the helpful Aurea as substitute for her rival in the story; Siegelinde Ohlssen proved to be responsive to suggestions and easy to direct and the Bonn students were thrilled to the teeth to be acting with her. It was Reisenfern who gave trouble.

"What the hell's the matter with him, Denmead? He's so wooden it isn't true." Whatmore ran his hands through his hair till it stood up like a golliwog's. "He's just walking through the part and he keeps going off the script."

"There's something wrong, certainly. Perhaps he isn't feeling well."

"Now I remember. This was the part he wanted played by a substitute in his clothes, you remember, I told you at the time. He suggested the stand-in could keep his back to the camera, if you ever heard such blasted rot. I thought I'd knocked the idea out of his head then."

"Perhaps he's not feeling well," repeated Denmead patiently. He was accustomed to having to offer his suggestions twice or even three times before Whatmore would notice them. "You'd better have a word with him and find out what is the matter."

Whatmore nodded and strode away.

"Look here, Reisenfern, what's the matter? These scenes are as flat as ditchwater, and it isn't the others, it's you. Aren't you feeling well?"

"Perfectly well, thank you. I am sorry—"

"And you keep going off the script and that upsets the others. How can they carry on with the dialogue if you keep on breaking it up?"

"I am sorry—"

"I can't have it. No, really, Reisenfern. You're wasting both time and film, and both cost money. You must pull yourself together and play these scenes as they are set down for you. I can't have—"

"But they're all wrong," said the Graf desperately.

"Now don't start that again, please. You are treating this girl as though she was made of pearl and gossamer and almost too holy to touch. You must remember that though she's very sweet and charming she's only a low-class innkeeper's daughter, practically a barmaid, and you are the Herr Graf von Grauhugel. She falls for you, but you don't, you are only amusing yourself with the wench, and—"

"How dare you!"

Whatmore instinctively backed away.

"Really, Reisenfern—"

The Graf mastered his temper. "That is what I meant just now when I said you had it all wrong. You see, he married her."

"What? Oh, nonsense. Sigmund never said that. He did say that she went off with him and was never heard of again, but as for marrying—"

"Sigmund knows nothing about it, but I do."

"How can you talk such rot! Sigmund is the Graf von Grauhugel with access to all the family archives and has heard all this story from his own family, after all, it is not so long ago—"

"Only eighty years."

"Exactly. Sigmund's father had the whole story from his grandfather who was this Graf Adhemar's brother. Now you come along out of nowhere with a name you admit to be assumed and say you know more about the family history than the family themselves. It's ridiculous."

"Is it?" said the Graf. He had begun to turn away and now looked back over his shoulder, one eyebrow a little raised and his mouth curling up at the corners. He was still in his actor's dress and Whatmore caught his breath, for the face which looked at him was exactly the face in the picture gallery labeled, in neat Gothic script, "Adhemar Hildebrand, Graf von Grauhugel, 1847-1869."

"You are one of the family," said Whatmore in a low voice. "There is no possible doubt about it."

"I have never denied it, if you think back. The only secret I keep is which one I am. Well, Herr Whatmore? Will you now accept that I may know what I am talking about?"

"But Sigmund—"

The Graf expressed, in a few vivid words, his doubts about the ultimate destination of Sigmund. "Let us not bother with Sigmund," he added. "Listen, Herr Whatmore. When the Herr Axenstrasse was here the other night, talking about making films, he was very insistent upon the importance of a happy ending. I have it right, yes?"

"Quite right. But we have—"

"And of a highly moral ending also? There must, he said, be wedding bells?"

Whatmore winced, for the point was painful. It is quite true that the public, and most particularly the American public, will not put up with a story which leaves the hero happy in anything lower than marriage and, even if they would, the production code administrator of the Motion Picture Association of America is there to see that they don't get it.

"I know," said Whatmore anxiously. "I put that point to Sigmund when we were talking about this story, but he was most insistent that there should be no marriage. You see, his point is this. There was a great deal of talk at the time about the Graf and the girl and the story is still remembered. She disappeared. She might have had a son. Sigmund says that if there is a marriage at the end of this film it might give someone the idea of coming forward with forged papers to claim the estate. It would be disproved, of course, but it would mean a great deal of trouble and expense. There was a famous lawsuit in England, called the Tichborne case, which cost the family many thousands of pounds to disprove."

"Of course," said the Graf, "no man of wealth and estates can ever be sure he will not be the prey of an impostor, but I think Sigmund is afraid of something more serious than that. He is afraid the story might be true."

There was a long pause.

"Reisenfern," said Whatmore at last. "Reisenfern, are you that man? The Graf Adhemar's legitimate heir?"

"He had no heir."

"You know that for a fact? Then what became of the girl?"

"She was drowned with him," said the Graf in a voice so low as to be barely audible. "They had been married for two days."

Whatmore made a small shocked noise and the Graf threw up his head.

"Well, there you are," he said in a cheerful voice. "You can have your wedding bells and the good public its happy ending and good morality too, and what is more, you will be telling the truth about a much maligned lady who cannot defend herself. I shall cease to be tiresome and everything will be—what was the Herr Axenstrasse's word? Hunky-dory?" He laughed.

"But," objected Whatmore, "how am I to satisfy Sigmund? He—"

"Refer the fellow to me," said the Graf, losing patience, and stalked out of the room.

Whatmore took a couple of turns up and down the room and then went to find Denmead.

"I gather," said the assistant producer, looking at him, "that things have not gone too well. Your hair looks as though you had been combing it with a rake. Tell uncle, then."

Whatmore did so, in full detail.

"You know," said Denmead, "you must hand it to Reisenfern, he's quite right."

"What about?" snapped Whatmore.

"Everything. Sigmund saying you mustn't end the film with a wedding for fear it should give someone ideas about claiming the estates is all poppycock. If there's enough money to be got, people don't need to have ideas suggested to them, they think them up for themselves. I wonder there hasn't been a Grauhugel Claimant long ago. No, Sigmund objects because he can't bear the idea himself. Did you ask Reisenfern if he could prove his statements? Because that's the point."

"No. I was just going to when he said 'Refer the fellow to me' and stalked off."

"Well, there you are. If Sigmund objects to the wedding bells, you can refer him to Reisenfern. I have great faith in that man, I have really. Look, Whatmore, you're not facing facts. If you don't have them married at the end, it's no good Axenstrasse promising to put your film on in his circuits because the American Film Control, or whatever they're called, won't allow it. Let that sink in."

Whatmore groaned.

"I've pointed this out before," pursued Denmead, "but you wouldn't listen. Now you've got to. Do you remember what happened to that excellent film *The Captain's Paradise* in America? They said it wasn't morally uplifting and that was that; the mere fact that it was brilliantly acted, magnificently produced, and incredibly funny cut no ice at all."

"Yes," said Whatmore miserably. "I mean, no."

"Put your shirt on Wedding Bells and they will bring home the bacon. Reisenfern will act like an actor instead of a petrified broomstick and everyone will be happy."

"Except Sigmund."

" 'Refer the fellow to me,' " quoted Denmead.

Chapter 14
NO SMOKING

BY WAY OF RETURNING the hospitality he had received at the castle, Elmer Q. Axenstrasse invited Whatmore and most of his company to see some of the rushes of the *Götterdämmerung* scenes which had been shot on the Rhine. After the showing there was a party with assorted drinks which everyone enjoyed except Whatmore, who left his forgotten and untasted while he discussed technicalities in a corner with Axenstrasse's assistant producer. Since the ladies of the company were there, Mrs. Axenstrasse was also present, a small plump woman with a wild-rose complexion, large blue eyes, and shining fair hair just beginning to silver. She was talking to Aurea Goldie and Siegelinde Ohlssen, who was wearing a large silver ring set with amethysts. It was so big that it covered the finger from the knuckle to the joint and was plainly very old.

"My dear Miss Ohlssen, what a wonderful ring!"

"It is not my own," said the German actress. "It is for me to wear for the time only, you understand? The Herr Reisenfern bring it for me for the film. Then I give it back I am sorry to say!"

"Is it your engagement ring in the film?"

"That is so. I wear it on this finger till we marry, then, after that, I wear it on my middle finger until my son takes a wife, and then she have it. That is, if I were in fact the Gräfin von Grauhugel, so the Herr Reisenfern tell me."

"It is beautiful," said Aurea. "I never saw it before. May I look at it?"

"She must not take it off," said the actor Reisenfern, "until I replace it with the wedding ring." He smiled at Mrs. Axenstrasse and addressed her in his careful English. "You like our Rhineland, madame? Is this your first visit?"

She said that it was and told him at some length how much she was enjoying herself.

"Your husband so busy," he said sympathetically, "it is a pity. You do not get *ennui*—bored—being so much alone?"

Mrs. Axenstrasse was quite accustomed to young actors making themselves agreeable to her in the hope of catching the eye of her husband; she was a sensible woman and knew how to deal with that sort of thing.

"Well, of course, it would be much nicer if Elmer—Mr. Axenstrasse-more time to go places with me, but I have a very dear friend of many years standing who is the wife of one of our generals over here. He is a busy man too, so she and I console each other and go to most places together."

"Very good," said the Graf, "very good. You visit together many beautiful places, interesting churches, historic museums, no doubt?"

"I just adore old churches and so does Delia. We visited your wonderful Cathedral of Cologne this morning. We were thrilled, Mr. Reisenfern."

The Graf paused momentarily to translate his thoughts.

"No doubt," he said, "you feel these things. I would say, a woman truly religious, no? You believe, I think."

"Oh yes! Back home I was brought up a strict Episcopalian, but of late years I have gained much strength and support from spiritualism. I take it you live hereabouts, Mr. Reisenfern, have you ever heard of Professor Xavier?"

"I have, yes. He has, I believe, some—some—"

"Reputation?"

"Reputation, that is it. I have never met him."

"He is a great man, Mr. Reisenfern."

"Indeed?"

"Yes. Yesterday my friend and I went to one of his séances and we are going again next Tuesday. Wonderful, wonderful. You should come, Mr. Reisenfern, indeed you should. At 9 P.M. I think I have one of his cards in my bag—have I? No—too bad. I will—"

"It is no matter. He is in Königswinter, yes? I can find out where."

"Mention my name. Do you really feel you would like to come?"

"If I can possibly," promised the Graf, "I will be there."

Having got what he wanted, he drifted away and eventually found himself at Axenstrasse's elbow.

"Ah, the Graf von Grauhugel in person. I am so glad to have you here. Have you got a drink? And what did you think of my little show?"

The Graf had not been listening to the conversations round him for nothing.

"Wonderful," he said, "wonderful. Amazing. Breathtaking. One of the greatest pictures ever made."

"Thank you, thank you. I hope you're right. But you're not drinking anything. Have a—"

"One moment," said the Graf, drawing him aside. "One private word, please. You know there is to be a séance on Tuesday next week at 9 P.M?"

Axenstrasse scowled.

"No, I didn't. Mrs. Axenstrasse tell you? Damn the man."

"Listen," said the Graf urgently. "You go too."

"What, me? Never. What d'you take me for? I wouldn't go to one of those—"

"Sh-sh! You go. I think you laugh, yes. Remember the clock? You go."

Axenstrasse stared and his face slowly cleared.

"What—you mean you're going to take a hand? Well, if anyone can do it it'll be you, I can see that clock yet."

"Then you will be there?"

"Let somebody try to stop me!"

"Not a word," said the Graf. "All most secret."

"Not a word," agreed Axenstrasse in a conspirator's whisper. "What you say goes."

"Thank you so much," smiled the Graf. "Most kind."

In the meantime, rehearsals and takes of the altered scenes—joint author, Johann Reisenfern—were in progress and Philip Denmead was delighted with them.

"What did I tell you?" he said. "Get a man on the job who knows his job and you're getting somewhere. Your friend the Graf Sigmund doesn't know the difference between a film script and a brochure about refrigerators."

Whatmore grunted. "I still don't know what I'm going to say to him."

"Don't say anything. Leave Reisenfern to do the talking. I say, that's a wonderful ring he had made for the betrothal ring, it must have cost him something."

"I suppose he picked it up in an antique shop."

"Oh no, that's impossible. It's a replica of the Gräfin's Ring of the Grauhugels. Old Klaus, the majordomo, nearly fainted when he saw it on Siegelinde's finger."

"It's an old one," said Whatmore.

"It can't be. Klaus told me about it, or rather, the original. You can see it in some of the ladies' pictures and there is a watercolor drawing of it in the catalogue of the Grauhugel treasures; Klaus showed it to me. It was lost when the Graf Adhemar was drowned."

"Oh, was it? I would have sworn this one was old. However, it's no business of ours. Did you tell Bert I want that scene of Franz with the wine bottles retaken? We can do it first thing tomorrow morning. It's got to be a dolly shot, that close-up, or it makes nonsense with the empty glasses."

The Graf and his servant went to Königswinter before the day set for the séance and familiarized themselves with the house both outside and in, with particular reference to the room in which the séances were held. It was a large room upon the ground floor and its windows looked out upon the street when the heavy violet curtains were not drawn across them. The room had something of the appearance of one in which board meetings arc held, for it was austerely furnished with a thick plain violet carpet on the floor, a bare polished table in the middle, and eight or nine upright chairs. There was also one large armchair for the medium in his trances, a corner which could be curtained off, and a handsome but perfectly normal console radio-gramophone.

It all seemed innocent enough, but the Graf and his servant were not satisfied with a cursory glance.

"This chair," said the Graf, referring to the large armchair, "must be even heavier than it looks. It will not move."

Franz went down upon his knees. "It is fastened to the floor," he said.

"Indeed. It is probably important that it should not be moved."

"There is a double wire passing from under the arm down one leg to the floor. It is like the wires used by the Herr Denmead's electrician, Harry, only black. Both black instead of one black and one red."

"Where does it go to?"

"I cannot say, mein Herr. Under the carpet, and from there who knows?" Franz felt about on the carpet with his hands and a movement in the middle of the room caught the Graf's eye.

"What did you do then? Do it again."

"A small lump under the carpet, Herr Graf. I pressed upon it like this."

"Most ingenious. When you do that the table rises a little and falls again. Part of the machinery. Is there a switch on the end of the black wire?"

"No, mein Herr. Only as it were a small box like a pillbox with two holes in it. I have seen Harry join lengths of wire to a box like that by means of a knob with prongs that fit the holes."

The Graf nodded. "No doubt there is something to be attached here. If we cut the wire, the activity, whatever it is, will cease, will it not? No, do not cut it now, Franz. Wait for the séance. Is there anything more to see here?"

There did not seem to be anything more and they were preparing to leave when they heard the front door open and shut. Then the room door opened and a man came into the room, a tall man, thin and dark, with a pale face and a small black pointed beard. He passed through the room without seeing anything, which was not surprising, though one would have thought that if he were really psychic he would have noticed something. He went through a further door and closed it behind him.

"The Herr Professor Xavier?" asked Franz.

"I assume so. Franz, did you post the letter I wrote to his sometime partner?"

"I did, mein Herr, yesterday. It is certain, is it, that the police were right in saying that this Professor had cheated that man?"

"Oh, I should think so, they seemed confident of the truth of the story. Besides, Franz, if two men are partners in a most successful fraud and one goes away full of money and changes his name while the other is glad to get a post as doorkeeper in a night club—whatever that may be—in Mainz, it does suggest that there has been no fair division."

"Certainly, mein Herr."

"Besides, if he does not come on Tuesday it does not matter, we can manage without him. I only thought that the poor man might like to meet his friend once more, you know."

Franz laughed. "I was wondering, by permission, what the doorkeeper would bring his old friend as a present. A nice box of cigars or a long knife?"

"You are right. Since there will be ladies here we must have no bloodshed. I wonder if I was wise to tell him."

"We can manage him, mein Herr, if we are ready for him."

"Let us go back to the castle, Franz, or we shall be missed."

Shortly before nine in the evening of the day fixed for the séance the company began to assemble, eight or nine in number. They were all English or American and women were in the majority. There were only three men present, a tall American with oddly light eyes and the slow nasal drawl of Texas, a small neat Englishman with a formal manner from the Army Pay Department who kept on biting his lower lip, and Elmer Q. Axenstrasse. He came in with his wife and her friend and behaved with the utmost decorum, rather as a man behaves who has been taken to a church service not of his own communion, with whose ritual and etiquette he is unfamiliar. He stood until he was encouraged to sit, meekly took his place at the table between his wife and her friend, and looked silently but searchingly about him. Mrs. Axenstrasse eyed him a little uneasily, but no one else took any notice of him. The large armchair was covered with a violet drapery, but otherwise the room was as the Graf and Franz had first seen it. The company waited in silence.

Presently the door at the far end opened and a boy, dressed like an Indian in white clothes and a turban, came noiselessly into the room and salaamed to the company. He glided round the room to the mantelpiece, which was bare except for a small lamp of Roman pattern, boat-shaped, with a wick at the bows. The boy produced a slightly inappropriate box of matches and lit the lamp; Axenstrasse thought how much more impressive it would have been if the lad had merely stretched out his finger to the lamp and a flame had appeared. Professor Xavier could benefit by a few hints on production. As soon as the flame burned up the boy switched off the electric lights and drew the curtains closely; the effect was to put the room in total darkness except for the weak and wavering flame of the Roman lamp. He slid silently to the door by which he entered, turned in the doorway, clapped his hands together high above his head and said, "The Master comes," in a high voice. He turned and vanished and once more there was silence broken only by the voice of Axenstrasse.

"Good," he said judicially. "Very good opening."

"Hush, Elmer," hissed his wife and nudged him.

"But I only said it was good."

"Hush. Be quiet"

Axenstrasse could only see, in the dimness, heads turned toward him, but the sense of disapproval was almost palpable. He relapsed into silence. Enough time passed for their eyes to become accustomed to the poor light; by the time Professor Xavier entered suddenly, unannounced, they could all see him well enough. He was dressed in a dark lounge suit, his beard covered most of the light triangle of shirt and collar under his chin, but his pale face showed up clearly, and his eyeballs shone in the lamplight. He came forward to stand by the corner of the table and began to speak; his eyes passed from one to another at the table and rested most, Axenstrasse noticed, upon himself. Probably the only stranger, and he was facing the light.

Xavier addressed them as "My friends," and spoke simply about the privilege of meeting together to seek knowledge and wisdom and courage. Even the American had to admit it was well done; the man had a pleasant voice and spoke good English. He went on to describe, "for the benefit of those among us who are newcomers to our circle," the form which the meeting would take. There would be music for a short period, during which they would all meditate together upon such lines as he would venture to suggest. Then they would all join hands upon the table and there might be a psychic manifestation which usually took the form of voices. Sometimes there were messages for individual persons, sometimes a general comment upon affairs. He himself might go into a trance, this usually happened but not always. He told them what to do and particularly what not to do if that happened. Above all, they were not to fear. Fear, in itself, was a harmful thing—

The voice was pleasant but a little monotonous and Axenstrasse soon became bored. From habit, without thinking what he was doing, he slipped two fingers into his breast pocket and took out one of the slim brown cigars he habitually smoked. He put it in his mouth and felt for his lighter, but before he could get it out a small flame appeared in the darkness and offered itself to the end of his cigar; the moment it was properly alight the flame went out.

The medium's voice faltered, paused for a moment; and then continued. Mrs. Axenstrasse laid her hand upon her husband's arm and pressed it menacingly. There was a metallic clatter upon the table and a brass ashtray arrived, conveniently placed for the American's use.

"Thank you," he said, and smiled widely.

Professor Xavier finished his preliminary remarks and then leaned across the table toward Axenstrasse.

"I am sorry, sir, to have to ask you to put that cigar out. I am quite sure that no discourtesy was intended, but discarnate spirits are known to be sensitive to scents of various kinds and tobacco—"

"One of 'em gave me a light, didn't he? I didn't light it."

"Well, apparently, but—"

"And brought me an ashtray."

"I think," said Xavier with a hint of strained patience, "that our new and welcome member does not quite understand. There are spirits and spirits, we do not wish to attract the wrong kind."

"But I like this kind," said Axenstrasse. "Good manners."

"Elmer," said his wife in a tone between entreaty and command.

"Please, sir," said Xavier, "please." He fixed his gleaming eyes upon Axenstrasse, who had, he was certain, produced both the flame and the ashtray. Probably come to make trouble. Would have to be watched.

"Oh, very well," said Axenstrasse, and laid down the cigar on the tray.

"Now, I think," said the medium, "we may perhaps counteract that smell with another more suitable to the circumstances."

He passed quickly round the table to light two or three joss sticks in a holder on the top of the cupboard, waving them in the air till they were glowing properly. Axenstrasse wrinkled his nose, for he detested the smell of joss sticks, and then suddenly noticed that the cigar in the tray before him had disappeared. He began to shake quietly with laughter; he had been promised fun and it had started.

Xavier moved on to the gramophone in the corner and switched it on; he watched it for a few moments and then closed the lid. The whisper of the needle was followed by the soft strains of solemn music and the medium returned slowly to the head of the table. Those joss sticks must be going well, thought Axenstrasse, there seemed to be a trail of smoke following Xavier as he went, only the smell was not that of joss sticks but much more like smouldering carpets.

Xavier clasped his hands slightly before him, not quite in an attitude of prayer but near it.

"Let us turn our thoughts toward the eternal verities." A pause.

"Truth. Truth in the heart and in the mind. Truth in asking and in answering. Truth in speaking and in hearing . . ."

The violins sang together.

"Wisdom." A long pause. Axenstrasse's neighbors at table had their eyes closed and a little frown of concentration between their brows; of all those facing the speaker only he was watching intently through half-closed eyes; surely the smoke was getting thicker? "Wisdom, worshipped by the ancients as divine; wisdom, our guide, our friend, our counselor. Let us ask advice how to act wisely for ourselves and others, so shall no emergency ever find us at a loss . . ."

Just below Xavier's elbow, down his side, a small glowing patch of red, clearing every moment. Axenstrasse's eyes opened wide.

"Look out, mister!" he cried. "Your pants are on fire."

Chapter 15
PROFESSOR XAVIER

THE MEDIUM XAVIER would greatly have preferred to have abandoned the séance at this point. Conditions, he would have liked to say, were unfavorable; there was evidence, he longed to add, of the presence of uncongenial and unsympathetic influences, and how right he would have been. He stood in the kitchen of his house, running the tap upon his smouldering coat pocket while the boy dashed upstairs to get him another coat, and considered the matter, eventually deciding to go on with it. For one thing, he was quite sure that the author of these disturbances was the film magnate, for Mrs. Axenstrasse had confided in him her grief at her husband's

prejudices. If one meeting could be broken up by such practices, the orga-
nizer would be greatly encouraged and there would be no peace at future
meetings. For another, if he disappointed his rather emotional clients,
they might not come again. Confidence in occult powers is a fragile growth
and easily withered.

On the other hand, if he went back now and carried on unperturbed,
he would have their sympathy and admiration. He could keep an eye upon
Mr. Axenstrasse, and he would, by heck!

He straightened his shoulders, slipped into the coat the boy held for
him, and strode masterfully back into the room from which he had so
precipitously fled.

"My friends," he said, with a hint of gentle amusement in his voice,
"I trust you did not allow that very absurd small contretemps to upset you.
Shall we now go straight on with the meeting as usual, or would you
prefer another short interval of meditation to compose your minds afresh?
I am in your hands."

"Let us go straight on," said a thin elderly woman, "shall we? We
have been doing as we thought you would wish, continuing our medita-
tions upon Wisdom."

There was a murmur of assent.

"You just carry right on, brother," said the tall Texan.

"Hear, hear," said the Englishman.

"Very well," said Xavier, "we will proceed as usual. Will you—"

"Attaboy," said Axenstrasse enthusiastically, since the last thing he
wanted was to have this delightful show come to a premature end, "attaboy,
Professor!"

"Elmer!"

"Thank you," said Xavier with a jerky bow. "Now, will you all draw
up nearer to the table, place your hands upon it, and each link your little
fingers with those of your next neighbors? Thank you, that is right." He
looked to make certain that Axenstrasse was effectually linked to his wife
and her friend on either side; he was. That would make sure of him since
the ladies were both devotees. Xavier sighed with relief and went to sit
down in his armchair, drawing the cover over his shoulders till only his
face was visible.

"Now," he said, "silence, please."

The silence grew and weighed upon them uneasily, one or two moved
restlessly in their chairs. Xavier in his low seat, deep in shadow, was all
but invisible, and moment by moment the tension grew.

Then the table became, as it were, alive. It quivered under the linked fingers of the company and became weightless, lifting a little from the floor and sinking gently again, since Xavier had his heel upon the knob under the carpet. Suddenly it rose in the air, throwing off the hands resting upon it, turned upside down, and was gently replaced with its legs upwards.

Xavier was horribly shaken, for Axenstrasse could not possibly have done this. It was true that the table was much lighter than it looked but, even so, it would have taken a man at each end to swing it over and replace it like that and Axenstrasse was sitting at one side. The medium sat up abruptly; this meeting must be stopped at once, he would switch on the lights, send the people away, and have a large brandy to steady his nerves.

But his clients were made of sterner stuff. Ecstatic murmurs of "Ah! Wonderful!" came to his ears. The Texan leaned toward him and asked in a loud whisper whether the table should be replaced right way up or did the spirits prefer it like that and the Englishman so far unbuttoned himself—he had never spoken at a seance before—as to say that since the spirit world was most probably in a quite different plane from ours, very possibly they did.

"Replace it, please," said Xavier in a weak voice as of one summoned back from a far place.

"They can always turn it over again," said Axenstrasse cheerfully, "if they like it better that way."

So it was put back on its legs again and thereafter showed no sign of life and once more the company waited.

At last the silence was broken by a deep sigh from somewhere near the fireplace. It was, actually, caused by Xavier blowing gently into the mouthpiece of his microphone to test it once again, but it had a most eerie effect and he himself answered it at once.

"Is there a spirit present?"

The answer came at once from the same place.

"Yes, indeed." A quiet voice not much above a whisper.

"Is it my control, Philibert the Christian?"

There was a light laugh and then—

"A Christian, yes, but not Philibert."

This voice had a strong German accent and its English was hesitant; Mr. Axenstrasse started and then began to shake with suppressed laughter. The ladies on either side of him tightened their grip on his little fingers.

Xavier's temper began to rise. This American was in the show business; was he also a ventriloquist?

"Who are you, please?"

"A friend of Truth and Honesty," said the voice with a hint of menace in its tones.

"That is very good," said Xavier, "but I think it would be better if you withdrew now, please, and gave way to my control. We know him."

"Without doubt," said the voice, "but I know you." There was another little laugh and this time Mrs. Axenstrasse drew in her breath sharply.

"Would it not," said the Englishman in a low tone, "be better to ask this spirit what he wants?"

"Thank you so much," said the voice graciously. "Most kind."

This time Mrs. Axenstrasse started violently; her husband disconnected their little fingers and took her hand firmly in his.

"Well?" said Xavier unwillingly. "What do you want?"

"The Herr Adolf Hirsch. Is he here? The Herr Adolf Hirsch. Surely he is here." The voice ran round the room as though someone were peering at the company in turn. "No? Strange, very. Ah"—as it reached the medium's chair—"here he is. You are the Herr Adolf Hirsch, *ja?"*

"I don't know what—" began Xavier.

"Oh *ja,* I think so. Your poor partner, he send me. After you went with all that so much money, he want you so much. Poor Gustav Nadler, you know. So poor he is but a doorkeeper in Mainz."

Xavier was almost fainting. Even if this was the American ventriloquizing, how could he know about Nadler, or the name Adolf Hirsch either? Surely there could not be anything in this spiritualistic nonsense after all—that table—

"Is Nadler dead?" he asked abruptly.

"What?"

Xavier pulled himself together.

"My poor old friend. Has he passed over?"

"I hope, not yet."

Xavier made a frantic attempt to regain control.

"I must ask you, please, to go away and give place to my control, Philibert. Philibert, can you come, please?"

"He cannot come," said the same voice, "he has a gumboil."

"A—?"

"Gumboil. He is sick in the face. Will not I do in place? I also am Christian."

"I should like to speak to Philibert, please," persisted Xavier.

"Oh, very well, you try."

Axenstrasse murmured something about a telephone and the lady called Delia hushed him fiercely.

"Philibert," said Xavier, "I am sorry if it is a trouble to you to speak today, but would you please tell us whether this spirit is true or false?" He lifted the mouthpiece of his microphone and spoke into it in the alleged Philibert's usual opening phrase. "Good evening, everybody. So nice we are all—"

He broke off abruptly because the reply did not come from the speaker hidden in the fireplace. It came direct from himself where he sat, and the heads of all his company turned round toward him like puppets jerked by a string. Xavier slid his fingers down by the arm of his chair; yes, the plug was firmly in the socket. He touched the wires running down from it, they were both loose and came up in his hand; the ends were clean, they had been cut, and the perspiration broke out on his forehead.

"You see?" said the German voice. "He cannot go on. He ask you, excuse him, please. He holds his poor face."

"May we say," ventured the thin spinster, "how sorry we are. We hope he will soon be better."

The unseen visitor laughed heartily and Axenstrasse joined in.

In the meantime there was activity of another sort going on outside. The little Hans and his friend Karl, aged thirteen and demons even for that diabolical age, had a standing feud with one of the Königswinter police, a middle-aged man who, with his wife, lived in a small house two doors down from Xavier's. The policeman's goat lived there also, tethered to a post in the garden.

"Luminous paint," said Hans to Karl, "shines in the dark."

"Why?" asked Karl.

"Because it does. If we were to paint the face of the policeman's goat, and her horns—"

"How?"

"We will feed her meal soaked in beer, then she will be mild and amiable."

"When?"

"On his evening off, which he spends in a café with his friends. Then, when he comes home and sees that face looking at him through the gate—"

Karl clasped his hands and jumped up and down.

Accordingly, upon the Tuesday night of Xavier's séance, two small boys made their way from their own homes to the policeman's garden. One carried a tin bowl of what looked like porridge and smelt like beer, the other carried a large tin of luminous paint and a small tin with a little black enamel left over from painting his bicycle.

"What for?" asked Karl.

"For finishing touches," explained Hans, who really had no very clear idea himself. "To pick out with black paint is always *modisch.*"

When they reached the policeman's house he had already gone out and his wife was indoors with the curtains drawn. The goat liked beer porridge . . . . At about this time Xavier's boy was announcing: "The Master comes."

The séance, proceeded rather jerkily after the news about Philibert's ailment. The invisible guest warded off enquiries about his identity after the company had insisted on his being heard.

"What is you name?" asked Xavier.

"Not Adolf Hirsch, at the least. What was yours in Amsterdam two years ago?"

"Where did you live, in life?"

"At home where I was born. I can see the place where you were born. A great building, it has high walls and many small windows. They have iron bars on them. I see the servants. They have clothes all alike and wear their hats in the house."

"What did you do, in life?"

"Unmasked rogues. What is that white under your coat?" It came out, unfolding, yard by yard. "It is like what girls dress in when I were young. Muslin, is it named? What for is it and why here?" It was gathered up in spite of Xavier's attempts to hold it, and tossed on the table. Mrs. Axenstrasse said "Oh my," under her breath.

"You brought it yourself," said Xavier, "please take it away again. I have no use for it"

"No? What is that black stick under your chair? The company most happy to see it, please. Oh, look, it comes out long and more longer. Beautiful." A thin telescopic rod, painted black, was laid across the muslin on the table so that it could be seen plainly, even in the dim light of the Roman lamp which appeared to be growing dimmer. This was not surprising. Xavier had calculated accurately the amount of oil required to last a certain time and then burn low; it was at this point that he usually "went into a trance" and produced visible manifestations.

"What you do with this, please? Walk muslin round the room like this, for ghost, *ja*?" Rod and muslin left the table to appear a moment later in a corner of the room, a tall thin apparition drifting vaguely about. "Look," went on the voice, "can you do like this? Look."

The exhibit crossed the room briskly from one side to the other, taking the table as it were in its stride. Mrs. Axenstrasse on one side and the tall Texan on the other felt it brush past their faces. The exhibit ended its act with a spirited dance on the hearthrug and then fell flat on the floor.

"You are a cheat, you know," said the voice. "Ghosts are not like that. How much money do people pay to see muslin on stick, eh?"

"This mockery must stop at once," said Xavier, struggling to rise. "My friends, as I warned you might be the case, we are the sport of a mischievous spirit. I shall turn on the lights and —"

"Hold him!" said the voice in German. "He is to stay there till I say he may move."

"By permission," gasped a second voice, "he is very violent. Mein Herr! An idea. May I remove part of his clothing?"

"Do so."

There was a confused struggle in the armchair which ended in Xavier wrapping himself tightly in the violet drapery; a moment later a pair of trousers, neatly folded, was laid in the middle of the table. Axenstrasse identified the garment, tossed it across to the Texan, and laughed until the tears came.

"Now," said the voice, reverting to its careful English, "is everyone happy, please? Or do I show some more small tricks?"

In the meantime Hans and Karl had made a workmanlike job of the policeman's goat in spite of the fact that she had kicked over the paintpot when they had only dealt with her head and horns.

"Oh, bad," said Hans reproachfully, "when there was quite a lot left."

"Bad," agreed Karl.

"But I don't know. I think she looks rather well. Oh, here's the black paint. Let's give her a pair of spectacles."

When this was done the effect was so striking that even the boys backed away.

"If I didn't know what that was," quavered Hans, "I'd be frightened."

"Untie her," said Karl.

"You untie her."

"No, YOU."

"Both of us," said Hans. "Come on."

So they unhooked the chain from the goat's collar and the ungrateful animal immediately chased them across the garden. They went over the fence like cats and the goat forgot about them, for she heard familiar steps coming along the road in front of the house. Master coming home. She trotted along the path at the side of the house to meet him, and the policeman's wife heard the patter of little hoofs on the concrete.

The policeman came slowly, looking over his shoulder as he did so, for there was an undersized little misery of a man hanging about outside Professor Xavier's house. His name was Gustav Nadler, though the policeman did not know it, and he was trying to summon up enough courage to try the door. He was so small and harmless in appearance that the policeman would not have given him a second thought but for the fact that anything to do with the professor interested him. He laid his hand upon the latch of his gate, heard a movement inside it, and looked round sharply. It was very dark just there and he was faced with a glowing spectral face of diabolical aspect, further bedeviled with large black spectacles, which hung in the air and stared at him.

The policeman clung to the gatepost with one hand and covered his eyes with the other; when he ventured to take another look there was nothing there. He staggered on to his front door and as he reached it his wife opened it.

"I think our goat is loose—what's the matter with you?"

"Nothing," said the policeman, sitting down heavily in the nearest chair. "What did you say?"

"I think our goat is loose. I heard her trotting on the concrete path outside and when I opened the back door there's a patch of light in the middle of the garden."

"Patch of light?"

She nodded. "On the ground. It glows, like."

The policeman, though still suffering from shock, was no fool and he had played tricks with luminous paint when he was a boy. He still did not want to go out into the dark and meet that face again, but he got up and went.

There was a patch on the ground which was certainly luminous paint but his goat was nowhere to be seen. This was not to be wondered at because dear little Hans had had another brilliant idea. The goat had returned from the front gate and was wandering across the garden toward the fence over which the two boys were leaning; the palely shining satyr face floated toward them.

"Looks like a ghost," said Hans, but he was wrong. No reputable ghost would think of looking like that.

"*Ja*," said Karl.

"I have it! The Herr Professor Something two doors along here likes ghosts. Deals in them, they say. Let's push her in at his back door. C'mon."

They entered the garden again, took the goat by surprise, and led her away out of the back gate and up the lane. They opened the wizard's back door, which was not locked since his "boy" had changed into normal clothes and slipped out for a drink. The goat, an obliging animal at heart, entered obediently, and the boys shut the door behind her.

Within the séance room one of the ladies had become a little hysterical and someone had suggested that perhaps a glass of water—

"Oh, certainly," said the disembodied voice. "Besides, it will be another little trick to show, *ja*? One little moment—"

The voice died away as though the speaker were moving toward the door leading to the rest of the house. The next moment there came, from beyond the door, the sound of a startled exclamation. *"Ach! Du lieber Gott!"*

Chapter 16
GRANDPAPA AMOS

WITHIN THE SÉANCE ROOM, a reversal of the usual order of things was taking place. The company who, as a rule, were awed, credulous, and a trifle quivery below the ribs were becoming increasingly cheerful, for Axenstrasse's open enjoyment was infectious. Besides, there is nearly always a subconscious feeling at mediumistic séances that one is probably being hoaxed and it is a relief no longer to have to suspend one's adverse instinct. "I always thought he was a twister," we say, and cheer up visibly. Xavier, on the other hand, had never believed for a single moment that any apparent psychic phenomena could be genuine; to him they were simply a means of raising money. Sometimes, when private interviews put him in possession of secrets which the original owners would much rather not have made public, he profited exorbitantly.

This time things were very different. At first he had been sure it was that irritating little American, but he soon had to abandon this idea. Axenstrasse could not have turned the table over; he might have produced the voice but he could not have walked the muslin round the room and still sat in his chair with his hands held. Who—or what—dragged the muslin from under Xavier's waistcoat, who cut the wires beside his chair, who produced that rod and, still worse, whose were the strong and yet impal-

pable hands which had first held him down and then so unseemly de-
bagged him? The voice, too, pleasant but mocking, and the knowledge it
held; horrible, all horrible. His breath came short and, though the perspiration ran down his face, he was cold. This, he said to himself, was the
last time, the very last time. Tomorrow morning early he would abandon
Köningswinter and spiritualism alike. Even burglary was better than this.
A glass of water arrived upon the table; it had been asked for and there it
was and the emotional lady was being encouraged to drink it.

"You know," said Axenstrasse, leaning across the table, "we'd have
done better to ask for cognac; I expect our friend would have brought it."

"Drinks on the house," said the Englishman, and there was a general
laugh.

"Certainly not," said the lady firmly. "I am a lifelong teetotaller."
She hiccuped suddenly and apologized and Axenstrasse laid his head on
his arms. Xavier suddenly lost his temper.

"The behavior of all of you is most unseemly," he said loudly.

"You started it, brother," said Axenstrasse.

"You—" began Xavier, but was interrupted by the light and laughing
voice which had tormented him before.

"Manners, manners," it said. "Nice behavior, please, in presence of
ladies. Now, I think I heard someone wish to see grandpapa. Not so?
Grandpapa's name Amos."

"Great jumping giraffes," said Axenstrasse, "my grandfather!"

"Your grandpapa, mein Herr? That is good. Just one moment. He come."

"Oh, Elmer," said his wife, and flung both arms round his neck. "Don't
let me see him!"

"It's all right, honey, I've got you and this gentleman won't let anything hurt you."

"Of course I would not," said the voice. "This entertainment all most
refined and harmless. The Herr Amos most well behaved. Look."

There, in the darkness, there shone a Face. It was whiskery and
bearded, it wore large black spectacles, and among the tangled hair on its
head there glimmered two neat little horns. It was quite high up because
its owner was standing on a chair.

The ladies screamed, even Axenstrasse gasped; for Xavier it was the
unbearable climax. He uttered a loud yell of terror, sprang from his chair
regardless of decorum, and made a rush for the door toward the street.

"It is the devil—the devil—"

Even as he rushed across the room the Face uttered a genteel snort
and the pointed ears came up; even as Xavier tore the door open and

rushed through it the Face bounded in pursuit of him. He flung the front door open; even as he set one foot upon the top step the Face caught up with him and, lowering its head, facilitated his departure after the manner customary with goats.

Axenstrasse disentangled himself from his clinging wife, tripped over the wizard's discarded violet drapery, and blundered to the door as a shot rang out in the street. He steadied himself and moved on to the outer door where his way was barred by a short-tempered animal with a phosphorescent head. Outside, there was heard the sound of running feet and a small man picked himself up from the ground and set off in pursuit. The goat leapt out of the doorway after the runners and the light of a street lamp fell upon her as she went.

"It's a goat!" cried Axenstrasse with a crow of laughter. "Oh—ha-ha-haa—my grandfather Amos a goat! And not far wrong, either!"

"Elmer!"

The policeman was walking slowly up the street, partly to look for his goat and partly to see if the little man were still hanging about. He was approaching the professor's door; he was in the act of lifting his hand to the bell when the door flew open and the wizard himself flew out. "He did not step out," said the policeman, describing the scene to his superiors later, "he did fly out. He came through the air and fell upon the stranger, who, being a small man and not robust, gave way beneath him and they rolled together. It was then that I observed my goat standing in the doorway and concluded her to be the cause of the offender Xavier becoming airborne. I then advanced toward the scene and observed the offender Xavier hitting the small stranger with his fist. I also observed the offender Xavier to be improperly dressed. I shouted out and the offender Xavier rose to his feet and, instead of stopping as ordered, ran away up the street. The stranger, still prone, then fired a small gun or pistol at the offender Xavier but missed him; he then got up and ran after him. My goat then vacated the doorway and joined in the pursuit, which all turned the corner by the chemist's and disappeared from sight. In pursuance of my duty, I went after them but, though I borrowed a bicycle which was outside a house, I did not see them again. With submission, I suggest that they attained the woods and probably climbed trees."

"Your goat also—"

"My goat returned later. There was, upon one horn, a small fragment of material resembling that used in the manufacture of gentlemen's underwear."

Axenstrasse, still laughing, returned to the séance room and switched on the lights; the company rubbed their dazzled eyes and looked about them. Professor Xavier had gone, the Face had gone. In their places were the actor Reisenfern bowing modestly by the fireplace and his wooden-faced servant stiffly on duty by the door. Axenstrasse greeted the Graf warmly.

"My dear Reisenfern! A brilliant performance—can't think how you did it—haven't laughed so much in years. Ladies and gentlemen, I don't know all your names so I can't do this job in proper form, but may I have the privilege and pleasure of presenting to you my young friend the Herr Johann Reisenfern, who is at the moment acting for a rival film company at the most romantic castle I have ever been privileged to visit. Reisenfern, that goat—"

"Ah, the goat was a—how do you say in business—a bonus issue? I do not know where she come from. I think somebody play trick on professor, you know? I give you my word when I go for glass of water and there is that in the passage, I was frightened, *ja.* I think I have raise real familiar spirit of professor, straight from Hell. Then I see it is goat, pity not to use her, *ja?* I hope the ladies not too much startled. Please forgive."

He was, of course, forgiven by almost all present; he was much too young, too charming, and too ingenuous for any normal person to bear a grudge against him. The one exception was the thin elderly spinster who waited till all the courtesies and congratulations were over and then rose to her feet, sweeping the company with a withering stare.

"I must be permitted to say that I do not agree. This evening's performance was a disgraceful and impertinent attempt by this callow play actor to discredit a man whose high character and spiritual gifts are quite beyond his comprehension. You ought to be ashamed of yourself!"

She walked stiffly toward the door glaring at the Graf, who bowed deeply and did not answer. When she had gone, he added: "I think I ought to say Professor Xavier not a nice man at all. The police suspect him of some things—" He sought vainly for words.

"Such as what?" asked Axenstrasse, deeply interested.

"My English is so bad—what is it when you know things about someone and say, 'If you do not pay, I tell'?"

"Blackmail, by thunder!"

"Oh, yes? And he cheat his partner, but that"—the Graf waved his hand carelessly— "not so important. Both bad." He smiled cheerfully. "All this here is a cheat. Look how he lift table." He demonstrated the knob under the carpet and Axenstrasse came gleefully to work it.

"Well," said his wife, "I am going to say one thing here and now, this is the very very last séance I ever attend. There!"

"Mr. Reisenfern," said her friend, "did you really do all those things that happened here tonight?"

"I and my servant, between us."

"Then, my dear young man, you and your servant should be on the stage. You'd be a riot."

"Thank you so much," said Reisenfern gratefully. "Most kind."

The company drifted away, leaving the Graf and his servant alone.

There was a folded piece of paper on the table which had not been there before and Franz unfolded it.

"What is this, mein Herr?"

The Graf glanced at it. "Ah yes. I saw some of these at the Herr Axenstrasse's party at Bonn. American money, a tip for you, Franz. A ten-dollar note."

"Is it worth anything in German money?"

The Graf had asked much the same question at Bonn.

"Forty-five marks, I understand."

The note disappeared into Franz's pocket.

"That cigar end burned through that coat surprisingly quickly, Franz. I had thought it would take much longer."

"I was blowing upon it, mein Herr."

"Very good. Now we can go home. If we should pass the Herr Xavier on the way, you have my leave to help the goat to chase him"

The scenes in which the German actress Siegelinde Ohlssen was engaged drew to their close with the indispensable wedding bells, faithful peasantry cheering, and village children strewing white rosebuds as the Graf and his bride walked out of the ancient church of Grauhugel village under triumphal arches to the music of the village band, heaven helping it, playing the "Wedding March" from *Lohengrin.*

"Once again," said Reisenfern to Whatmore, with a laugh, "you are all wrong, but this time it is not important, it is only the place that is wrong. You have, at least, got them respectably married and that is the main thing."

"Where were they married, then?" asked Whatmore. "At a registrar's office?"

"Please?"

"Or don't you have them in Germany?"

"You mean the civil ceremony, at the Bürgermeister's office? Oh yes. We have both, the civil ceremony and the religious, usually but not necessarily on the same day."

"I see. Where were they married?"

"At the church of a small village outside Heidelberg, very early on a June morning. It was still fresh and cool before the heat of the day and all the birds were singing and the air full of the scent of roses. The minister was so old he was nearly blind, but he knew the service by heart so it did not matter. The witnesses were the landlady and her family from the inn where Cecilie stayed for a day or two before the wedding; the two smallest children scattered, not roses, but rose petals, down the path to the gate. Someone in the village had white fantail pigeons, which came down and walked like bridal attendants in front of the bride. They were not at all afraid, they ran about on their little coral feet among the pink and white petals, picking them up; then at the gate they all rose up in a flock and flew away. Curious, that."

Whatmore waited for more, but the actor Reisenfern seemed to have retired into some private dream.

"The bridegroom," said Whatmore eventually, "does he not have to be accompanied by some witness who knows him?"

"Oh yes. Particularly at the civil ceremony where all the signing is done. The witness in this case was the bridegroom's cousin, young Konrad von Grauhugel of the Polish branch of the family; he also was at Heidelberg at that time."

"They why did not he come forward and say that there had been a marriage?"

"Because he was killed in a duel two days later. Pistols," said the Graf, frowning. "As I told the Herr Axenstrasse when he was here, pistols are horribly dangerous."

"And he had told no one—"

"No. He had been asked not to; the-the Graf Adhemar preferred to tell his family himself. It would not do, you see, for the news to reach them by way of rumor."

"You know," said Whatmore, "that's a terribly good story—"

"What do you mean," said the Graf sharply, "a good story? Anyone would think you did not believe it."

"Am I supposed to? How could you know all that unless you were there?"

"That is certainly a point."

"But I do like your description of the wedding. I think my version of it is better cinema, but I wish I'd thought of the white pigeons."

Siegelinde Ohlssen, changed into ordinary clothes, came out to them.

"Are you satisfied with that, Herr Whatmore?"

"We'll see the rushes tonight to make sure, but I think they will be all right."

"Because, if you do not need me any longer, I ought to go home tomorrow; I have to start rehearsing for *The Twilight Lover* next week and I want to spend a few days with my mother first."

"Certainly, *gnä'* Fräulein. I will let you know definitely as soon as I have seen the rushes tonight, will that do? I have also to try to tell you," said Whatmore, to whom graciousness never came easily, "how immensely I am—we all are—in your debt for all you have done for us and the way you have worked with us. No one could possibly have been more helpful and cooperative—"

"Or more brilliant in your part," interrupted the Graf. "The way the *gnädiges* Fräulein brought out the underlying innocence and purity of Cecilie, in contrast to her rather boorish environment, I found most touching. I thank you from the bottom of my heart."

"It was nothing. You showed me how to read the part and I merely carried out your ideas. And now," she took hold of the ring on her left hand, "I suppose I must very reluctantly return this lovely thing; I had been hoping you would forget about it."

"Fräulein, I only wish I could, but it is not mine to give. It is, in truth, only borrowed. Thank you a thousand times; the ring will always have an additional luster for me because one so lovely and so gracious has worn it." He took it from her and slipped it on his own finger.

"Now I must go and pack if I am to leave tomorrow. I shall be very sad to leave all this dignity and peace. I shall see you all later, yes?" She turned and walked up the steps to the entrance and disappeared, and the Graf watched her out of sight before turning away.

"Reisenfern, just a moment. May I look at that ring?"

"If you wish," said the Graf slowly, and gave it to him. Whatmore examined it closely.

"This is very old," he said.

"Very old."

"And very like the Gräfin's Ring of the Grauhugels. I have seen the picture of it in the catalogue."

"Oh, yes?"

"Were there, then, two of them?"

"No. Only one."

"Then where did you get this one from, Reisenfern?"

"I am sorry, I cannot tell you."

"You cannot mean you don't know?"

"Of course not. I meant what I said, that I cannot tell you."

"You won't, you mean."

"If you prefer it," said the Graf coolly. "Moreover, if I did you would not believe it."

"I heard that it was lost when the Graf Adhemar was drowned, is that correct?"

"To be strictly correct, it was lost when the Gräfin Cecilie was drowned. She was wearing it, as was her right."

"And I suppose that the body was found and not recognized, is that right? That is, if you know, though I can't imagine how you could."

"That is perfectly correct," said the Graf in a wooden voice.

"Someone then found it and eventually it came to your notice, perhaps in a curio shop, and you recognized it and bought it, is that right?"

"No. You heard me tell the Fräulein Ohlssen that it was not mine, it was borrowed."

"Then someone else bought it!" said Whatmore in a tone of rising exasperation, for he felt that he was being played with.

"No. Herr Whatmore, why are you becoming so heated about this ring? Surely, with perfect courtesy, it is no concern of yours."

"Because, if this is really the original ring, surely the Graf Sigmund ought to have it and he is a friend of mine."

"I see," said the Graf. "In the meantime—thank you—" He held out his hand for the ring.

"I am not at all sure that I ought to part with it," said Whatmore undecidedly. "You admit it is not yours and I should never forgive myself if it disappeared again."

"It will not, I assure you, unless I disappear also," said the actor Reisenfern pointedly, and Whatmore came down, as it were, to earth with a bump. There was still several days' work to do on the film, mainly retakes of parts of scenes in which Reisenfern appeared, and here was Whatmore exasperating his principal actor into leaving him at a moment's notice on account of a quarrel over something which was no personal concern of his. The film—

"I am a fool," he said half aloud, and the Graf smiled faintly.

"No, no, my dear Whatmore. On the contrary, your sentiments do you credit and Sigmund ought to be most grateful. My ring, please."

Whatmore gave it to him.

Late that night, when the rushes had been seen and approved and everyone else had gone to bed, Whatmore sat in his room writing a long letter to the Graf Sigmund von Grauhugel, student of metallurgy at the University of London.

Chapter 17
THE GRÄFIN'S RING

WHILE THE GRAF was engaged in acting his love scenes with the innkeeper's daughter, Franz, not being required on the set, had an unusual amount of time at his disposal. He would mount his glittering new bicycle, ride very carefully down the steep and twisting drive, pass rapidly and without stopping through the village of Grauhugel and out into the country beyond. It was his own business where he went in his spare time and, since he said nothing, his master made no comment.

Three days later he was once more on the set, not taking part since he was not needed but unobtrusively in the background watching all that went on and giving a helping hand to the cameraman and the stagehands. He was there again the next day, and the next.

"You have tired of cycling, Franz?" asked the Graf.

"A little, mein Herr. Besides, there is nowhere very interesting to go. I have seen all these villages."

"No doubt, but I thought that you spent your time with friends."

Franz shuffled his feet.

"Herr Graf—"

"Well?"

"By permission, I think I must be getting old! I do not look old, I do not feel old. But—but I am not interested any more. These girls, they are very friendly, very pretty, but, mein Herr, how they weary me! They look at me sideways and laugh, and I tell them to go back to their mothers and find something useful to do. Herr Graf, our Rhineland girls used not to be like that when I was here before. They had charm." Franz sighed deeply. "There is something lacking in these modern girls. They are like pretty pictures, you look at them, you admire, and then you walk away. It is very sad for our Rhineland that its girls should be without charm."

"You dunderhead, Franz!" said his master, laughing. "It is you in whom there is something lacking, not these girls."

"What? The Herr means that I am not really flesh and blood? How

sad, mein Herr. I am deeply sorry for Franz Bagel, who is no longer interested in pretty girls. It is a tragedy, by permission."

"It is, Franz," said the Graf soberly, "and you threw your manhood
away for me."

Franz's face brightened. "Then I have the best of the bargain after all,
for there are so many girls and only one Herr Graf. Besides, they all grow
old and wrinkled and have shrill voices and complain of rheumatism and
ask for money to buy things with. Even I might have had rheumatism and
toothache and gone bald. I should hate to go bald, mein Herr. Oh no,
things are much better as they are."

The filming of Whatmore's picture drew to its close and the cast began to turn their minds to the future, since in a few days' time most of
them would be back in England; all of them, in fact, except the extras
from the village. These men and women were frankly cast down and openly
lamented the end of their engagement.

"How dull everything will be," said the girls. "We shall not know
what to do with ourselves when they have all gone."

"You can do some useful work for a change," said their mothers,
"and no nonsense about you can't scrub the floor, it will spoil your hands."

"But it paid much better than scrubbing floors, Mother."

"Too well paid, you were getting spoilt. Now go and wash your father's
shirts for nothing, and don't put that face on at me. You were a good
obedient child before you took up with all this, Trudi, now don't make me
regret I let you do it. The soap is on the shelf above the fireplace."

Aurea Goldie, strolling on the terrace with the actor Reisenfern, was
saying much the same thing as the Grauhugel girls.

"I am sorry it is nearly over, I have been so happy in this wonderful
place."

"I am glad you have been happy, *gnä'* Fräulein. This place suits you,
I think, you look at home here."

"I wish I were! Tell me, Herr Reisenfern, when you leave here, where
do you go? Shall I see you in London?"

"I shall not be coming to London, no. I have one more thing to do and
then I go home to my wife, *um Gottes willen."*

"Is it long since you saw her?"

"Far too long, but not, I think, much longer now. Tell me, Fräulein,
do you know if the Herr Whatmore has written to the Graf Sigmund in
London to come here?"

"He has, yes." Since Whatmore had told her that he had sent for Sigmund "to get the truth out of this mystery merchant," the question was a little embarrassing.

"And he comes?"

"Tomorrow."

The Graf heaved a long sigh of relief. "That is good. Very good. I want to speak to him."

"I am not sure that I do," said Aurea abruptly and the Graf was surprised.

"May I know why, Fräulein?"

"I know him very well; I have known him for a long time, all the time he has been in London. I—that is, I mean that is why I came here, to see this place. When I heard that George Whatmore was making a film here, I joined the cast for that purpose."

"I see," said the Graf, "or do I? Why does he not live here?"

"I don't know," said Aurea.

"You are troubled, Fräulein."

"I am, yes. I like him very much," she said, facing the Graf squarely. "He asked me to marry him sometime in the future when he should have got a good post in America and his future was assured. I don't understand! He is quite well off, he admits he could afford to live here. Why does he want to go to America to work and let this place as a hotel or something horrible?"

"He wants to turn this place into a hotel?" said the Graf in an angry voice. "He has duties here. Is the man mad?"

Aurea shook her head. "I refused him. I said he was too modern and materialistic. I cannot respect a man who thinks of nothing but money."

"Of course you could not, the mere idea is repugnant. I myself, also, have something to say to him," added the Graf as though talking to himself. "I am glad he comes tomorrow. It is rather funny, this. The Herr Whatmore has got him here to unmask me, you knew that? Yes. And there is nothing more I want in life than to meet Sigmund. I produced that ring on purpose to give Herr Whatmore something to distrust me about; I tried several times but he thinks of nothing but his film, does he? It took the Gräfin's Ring of the Grauhugels to make him take a little notice of me, as a man I mean, not as an actor. Very funny."

"Is that really the original Gräfin's Ring? Truly?"

"Truly it is," said the Graf, smiling at her. "Are not you, also, going to ask me where I had it from?"

"No, I don't think I am." She looked him straight in the eyes. "I am not going to—to ask anything about it. I—" She stopped, and fell back on the formal phrase. "I am so very glad to have met you." She held out her hand and he bowed over it and kissed it, just as a deep metallic roar boomed out from the castle. "That is the dinner gong, we must go in."

"I am your servant, Fräulein." said the Graf, "now and always."

The Graf Sigmund, in his Bloomsbury lodgings, pushed his textbooks away from him and reread for about the tenth time the letter from George Whatmore which he had received the night before, and his mind went back to the day when he had first heard of the innkeeper's daughter from Heidelberg.

He was about fifteen years old, the only child of the Graf Kaspar Leopold, and he had grown up knowing, from infancy, that he was somebody very important, as indeed he was in the small Grauhugel world. He was the heir to the castle and the lands around it; the armorial bearings carved over the doors and engraved upon silver and glass were his own; the suits of mail in the upper hall which used to frighten him when he was a baby had been worn by his forefathers, he knew all their names. He was equally familiar with the long roll of his family history; this man followed Barbarossa to the Crusades, that one fought in Switzerland for Maximilian I, that other was killed at Rossbach in 1757 when Frederick the Great so resoundingly defeated the French. These men were gallant and staunch and earned the respect of men of their day—Sigmund averted his mind from his great-great-grandfather Stanislaus—and he, Sigmund, in his own person, represented them in the world of today. He was, himself, Maximilian and Sigismund, Roland, who fell at Valmy in 1792, and grandfather Rudolf, who fell at Ypres, and someday he, too, would be Graf von Grauhugel.

Then, in the winter of 1938 Sigmund fell sick with jaundice and was kept indoors for some time after he was well enough to be out of bed, because the weather was so bitter and it is a mistake to catch a chill on the top of jaundice.

He spent much of his time in the library reading history with special reference to the von Grauhugels; when he had exhausted that line he read old documents inscribed in crabbed Gothic script on yellowed parchments with a peculiar smell all their own. He soon tired of these because they were really very dull and the lettering made his eyes ache. He unlocked some drawers he did not remember ever having opened before and found some correspondence of the middle 1800s. Some of these were most amusing and for the first time he felt a gleam of sympathy for the errant Graf

Stanislaus. Beatrix, of the princely house of Wittelsbach, was certainly a
terror.

Then he found an envelope endorsed "Death of the Graf Adhemar
Hildebrand 1869" and drew out its contents.

Half an hour later, with a white face and trembling knees, he burst
into his father's study where the Graf Kaspar Leopold was reluctantly
engaged with estate accounts. He disliked mathematics.

"My father—"

"Yes, come in—what is it, Sigmund? How ill you look, have you
caught cold?"

"No, no, I am perfectly well. My father, have you ever read these?"

The Graf Kaspar glanced quickly through the handful of letters and
memoranda which the boy thrust at him.

"I looked through them many years ago, I am not sure that I ever read
them very carefully. Why?"

"Why? Because it says there, in that letter, that the Graf Adhemar
told the writer that he was going to marry that girl Cecilie Gutmann, the
daughter of a tavern-keeper, and that—"

The Graf held up one finger and Sigmund fell silent.

"It also says, if you have read it through, that he was drunk at the time
and subsequently denied having said anything of the sort."

"But if he wanted to keep it a secret and he found he'd let it out, of
course he would deny it. The girl disappeared when he did and he was
drowned a few days later. What was to stop him—"

"Sigmund. If you are still suffering from fever I think you had best go
back to bed for a few days until you are completely restored. You look
very unwell to me."

"My father, I am perfectly well, I thank you. It is this news which—"

"News? What news? I have heard none. Sigmund, how dare you take
this tone to me? Do you suppose that I and my father and my grandfather
are all fools?"

Sigmund stammered apologies and his father went on..

"All this story was very carefully inquired into at the time and no
proof whatever of its truth could be found. It is true that Adhemar was
said to be dangling after this young woman at Heidelberg at that time and
that was not a very creditable thing to do since he was then betrothed to
an English lady, a Miss Crompton from Lancashire, with a great deal of
money. A very charming young lady, too, my grandfather told me, he
remembered her very well. She was staying here, in the castle, when the
tragedy happened. Adhemar was on his way home from Heidelberg and

for some reason decided to perform the last part of the journey by river. It was all most unfortunate."

"But Cecilie Gutmann——"

"I have never stinted or circumscribed your reading in any way, Sigmund, and I always thought you were reasonably intelligent. You are very young, but it must surely have dawned on you by now that men do not always marry the young women with whom they are so ill-advised as to philander. Especially if the young woman is of a much lower social order. As in this case. Adhemar was very young and very likely would have settled down, but he was certainly wild and irresponsible at that time. All the same, I refuse categorically to believe him so lost to all sense of family dignity as to marry the daughter of a tavern-keeper named Gutmann. The thing is just not possible."

"But if they lived together and she had a son——"

"I perceive that you have learned something from your reading. Then the son would be illegitimate and we need not bother about him."

"No. But—forgive me, my father——"

"Go on," said the Graf resignedly. "Better get it all off your chest and have done with it. What is it?"

"With submission, all you have said only shows that a marriage was improbable. Not that it was impossible. Nobody seems to know where he was for four days, from the day he left Heidelberg till the day he was drowned. They might have gone somewhere and——"

"Fiddlesticks," said the Graf impatiently.

"My father. Was she very pretty?"

The Graf hesitated, but he was habitually truthful and habit is strong.

"My grandfather said that a man who knew her told him that she was like sunrise on a morning in May."

"Oh dear," said Sigmund.

"Sounds a bit chilly, to me," said the Graf, briskly overtaking his error. "You know, frost on the glass and a nip in the air. What?"

Sigmund smiled wanly.

"Another thing," said his father, pursuing his advantage. "If a girl like that had married the Graf von Grauhugel, do you suppose her family wouldn't be all cock-a-hoop about it? Of course they would. Tell all the neighbors——"

"Perhaps she did not tell them," said Sigmund.

"Oh, double fiddlesticks."

"Finally——" said Sigmund, producing his ace of trumps.

"Thank heaven for that!"

"—finally, my father, where is the Gräfin's Ring?"

This remained the one insoluble lump in the gravy which even the Graf Kaspar could not smooth away. It disappeared at the time that the young Adhemar went to Heidelberg for the last time and had not been seen since.

"But would not his mother, Beatrix von Wittelsbach, have worn it until Adhemar was betrothed?" asked Sigmund. "In that case, surely Miss—Miss Crompton should have had it?"

The Graf Kaspar laughed aloud and then checked himself. "The loss of that historic ring was no laughing matter," he admitted, "and every subsequent generation has grieved about it as you are grieving now, Sigmund. What happened was this, as my grandfather described it. On the day before Adhemar went away that last time, his mother gave him the ring to give to the English miss, and that evening, my grandfather said, they were all told to keep out of the young couple's way and give Adhemar a chance of presenting it in proper form. So they all scattered about the castle, my grandfather and his two brothers and three sisters, to keep out of Adhemar's way. But he kept on turning up here and there, in the gun room, out in the stables, or up in his sisters' boudoir, and none of them liked to ask whether the deed had been done because they weren't supposed to know about it. The gift of that ring was considered to be nearly as binding as a marriage. Well, the evening passed on and the English miss excused herself and went to bed early with what she said was a headache, but I should think was a fit of pique with Adhemar for spending the evening avoiding her. Or perhaps they had a quarrel, I don't know. Everybody hoped, of course, that she had retired in an access of maidenly bashful delight. However, next morning Adhemar was not to be seen and on inquiry it appeared that he and that servant of his, Franz Bagel, had saddled horses and ridden out of the gate just before four in the morning. As soon as it was light, in fact. The Gräfin Beatrix was greatly incensed; naturally, I think; when she found out that poor Fräulein Crompton had not been given the ring the temperature rose several degrees, and when a thorough search of Adhemar's rooms failed to produce the ring, so, presumably, he had taken it with him, she was beside herself with fury and everyone fled and hid themselves. The majordomo, our Klaus's grandfather, ventured in with a tray of soup or something at about midday and she threw a seven-branched china candlestick at him and it went into a thousand pieces. You know the fellow one, it is in the drawing-room. Pink roses and cupids. They came from the English Prince Consort's Great

Exhibition of 1851. My grandfather said it's a wonder the castle didn't catch fire with spontaneous combustion."

"*What* a blowup," said Sigmund appreciatively.

"Yes, indeed. The boys kept out of the way and the girls took turns in sitting with Miss Crompton and holding her hand. About ten days later the news of the tragedy reached the castle, and that, of course, capped everything."

"And great-grandfather inherited the title."

"That's right. Miss Crompton went back to England and married a man named Blinks or Binks. I remember the name because apparently the Gräfin Beatrix walked up and down the passages here, wringing her hands and saying 'But what are Binks?' You see, she hoped my grandfather would marry the girl in place of his brother, Adhemar. Well, my boy, that's a long page of not very edifying family history which you've never heard before."

"Thank you very much for telling me," said Sigmund. "I think most of it is frightfully funny, but I'm glad I wasn't there."

"I am entirely with you on that point."

"It doesn't seem," said Sigmund after a moment's thought, "that Adhemar was frightfully keen on this English girl."

"Well, no, but she really was extremely nice and pretty into the bargain and, besides, there was all that money. A man owes a duty to his family, you know."

"Yes, indeed I do, my father. But—"

"More buts! What this time?"

"If he took the Gräfin's Ring away with him, doesn't it look as though he meant to marry Cecilie Gutmann?"

The Gräfin Beatrix had been in her ornate tomb for more than seventy years, but her temper had been handed down to most of her descendants and it sprang to life at this point. Sigmund bowed to the storm, crept away as soon as possible, and never raised the subject again though it was seldom far from his mind. If Adhemar had married the girl and if she had had a son . . . .

Now there had arisen this fellow Reisenfern, whose name was not Reisenfern, who was the image of the Graf Adhemar and who had the Gräfin's Ring.

Chapter 18
THE GRAF SIGMUND

MOST OF WHATMORE'S English actors had already packed up and left for home before the Graf Sigmund came. Like the instrumentalists in Haydn's "Farewell" Symphony, they finished their parts and closed their scripts, as it were blew out their candles and one by one stole away, and the tall castle grew quiet and empty and withdrawn. On the day when Sigmund came the last retakes had been shot and the last rushes shown and passed. Bert, the cameraman, spent the day packing his cameras and other equipment into padded wooden cases; Harry, the electrician, labored all day winding up incredible lengths of rubber-covered wire upon small drums, dismantling kleig and floodlights, and removing switches. The great hall accumulated a stack of boxes, suitcases, and trunks to await the van which would convey them to Cologne Station in the morning. Toward evening of the day when Sigmund came, Aurea Goldie was not to be seen and it was understood that she was up in her room with her maid, Lily, packing. Reisenfern and his servant were also closeted in their room, but no one knew what they were doing. Klaus pattered about with a pale abstracted face, avoiding speech with anyone except the underservants whom he continually drove to fresh outbursts of cleaning, tidying, and clearing up.

Toward the time when Sigmund was due to arrive, Whatmore was seized with the most intolerable fidgets, mainly due no doubt to the end of the long strain of producing the picture; rehearsing the actors, overseeing every take, arranging the lights, the grouping, the action, scrutinizing the rushes, criticizing, amending, altering. Denmead had done more than his share of the work, but Whatmore was a man who did all his worrying himself. Now that the film was finished, he worried about Reisenfern.

Denmead strolled down the steps into the castle court and found Whatmore pacing slowly back and forth across the entrance gate, watched by the porter from the window of his room.

"Melancholy, all this," said Denmead, "isn't it? I shall be thoroughly sorry to go, but now we've finished I'd like to leap into a car and drive rapidly away. Last nights are always beastly."

"Well, you can," said Whatmore.

"Can what?"

"Leap into a car and drive away. I can manage, I've got the two men still."

"What's the matter with you?" asked Denmead.

"Nothing. Where's Reisenfern?"

"In his rooms, I suppose. Why?"

"Because," said Whatmore, "there's another quarter of an hour before Sigmund is due and if Reisenfern chooses to walk down those steps, across the court, and away out of sight I don't see how I'm going to stop him."

"I'm quite sure you could not," said Denmead with emphasis, and added in a lighter tone: "Is that why you're quarter-decking in front of the gateway, to stop him if he comes out?"

"Some such idea," muttered Whatmore. "You see, I—"

"Are you proposing to hurl yourself at him in a Rugby tackle, get him down and sit on his head? The servants would kill you."

"Yes, and why? Who is this fellow, Denmead? There's a mystery about him and I want to know what it is."

"Why worry? It isn't your mystery. Leave it to Sigmund."

"And Aurea looks at him as though he was a visitant from Mars or somewhere."

"Awed wonder mingling with motherly instincts?"

"You've hit it exactly, Denmead. Why?"

"Come in and take a couple of aspirins," said Denmead soothingly.

"Get—are you laughing at me? I know how much I owe you, but—"

"Listen. There's a car coming."

The porter ran out to stand at attention by the gate and the two Englishmen went back to the steps. At the head of these Klaus was standing with his wand of office in his hand and two footmen behind him. On the other side of the door stood the housekeeper, a stout woman in black silk. Denmead glanced up at the windows above and caught a glimpse of Aurea's golden hair against a curtain, but no one looked out from Reisenfern's suite. There was a scatter of gravel and a car swung to a stop, the footmen leapt down the steps to open the door, and the Graf Sigmund stepped out, a tall dark man with a saturnine expression, a long scar down one side of his face, and his brows drawn together.

"Whatmore! Glad to see you. How are you? I want a word with you if you don't mind." Denmead, seeing that he was not wanted, stepped back and Sigmund went on in a low tone. "Is that fellow Reisenfern still here?"

"I believe so," said Whatmore. "In his room, I understand."

"Good. I should like a few words with you before I have him down, one or two points I'd like to clear up. Come indoors." Sigmund walked up the steps with Whatmore a pace behind. At the top Klaus offered three enormous keys on a hammered iron ring eight inches across; Sigmund touched them symbolically, spoke to the old man, and laid a hand for a moment on his shoulder. Whatmore stopped dead in his tracks, staring. What a scene, what a moment, what a shot. Why the heck couldn't somebody have told him that there was this little ceremony when the Graf came home? The housekeeper curtseyed and Sigmund spoke to her also, calling her by name, and then walked in through the great doorway. Whatmore followed, wondering whether even now he could not get Reisenfern down to do that last shot before everything broke up, but the cameras were all packed—

"Come in my study," said the Graf Sigmund. "Klaus! Whatmore, a glass of sherry or what? There's a Malaga which I rather fancy, will you join me? Klaus, the Malaga. Now, Whatmore. Tell me again where this fellow came from; when and where did you first meet him?"

Whatmore embarked upon the story of that summer morning when Victor Beauregard fell down the stairway and two young men walked up the steep and winding drive to the castle gate. He had not proceeded far with the story when Klaus came back with a salver, two wine glasses, and a decanter; Whatmore broke off until they should be private again. Klaus served the wine, set the decanter on the table, and stepped back.

"By permission, Highborn—"

"What is it?"

"The Herr Reisenfern presents his humble duty to the Graf von Grauhugel. He begs the favor of a short interview with the Graf Sigmund in the Herr's room."

"What! The insolent fellow dares to send for me! Which room is he in?"

"In the Graf Adhemar's suite, if it please the—"

"It does not please me at all. Who the devil put him in there?"

Klaus took another step back and Whatmore said that actually he didn't think anyone put Reisenfern there, he just— But as quite evidently neither master nor man had heard a word of what he was saying, he left the sentence unfinished.

"Send the footman up and let them bring him here to me," said the Graf Sigmund.

Klaus turned two shades paler but stood his ground.

"By permission, if the Herr Graf would let his old servant speak—"

"Well, get on. What is it?"

"I and mine have served many generations—"

Sigmund's fingers played a little tattoo upon the table; Klaus swallowed and started again.

"With deep respect, the Herr Reisenfern is—is no ordinary man."

There was dead silence for a moment before Sigmund spoke again. Then, in a voice suddenly grown flat and tired:

"Klaus. Did you also see that ring?"

"Yes, Highborn."

"Klaus, my old servant. Who is this man?"

The majordomo shook his head in silence and at last Sigmund rose to his feet.

"I suppose I had better go up and see him," he said, and walked heavily out of the room, but by the time he reached the great stairway his head was high again and his jaw set. Not for nothing was the von Grauhugel motto the one word "Tenacity."

He strode along the passage to the door of the suite occupied by the Herr Reisenfern, flung the door open, and walked straight in. It was a large room with two wide windows through which the setting sun was streaming; at the further end of it, facing him in a high-backed chair with the arms ending in eagle's heads, there sat the duplicate of the portrait of the Graf Adhemar Hildebrand in the picture gallery. He wore the dress of the 1860s, his hands lay along the arms of the chair, and his feet rested upon a footstool; behind his chair stood his servant, Franz Bagel, stiff in attitude, wooden in expression, and looking at nothing in particular.

"What is this mummery?" demanded the Graf Sigmund. "I understand that you are a film actor, but the Herr Whatmore tells me that your engagement has now been terminated."

"Franz," said the Graf Adhemar, "the door."

Sigmund had left it wide open; Franz walked across, deliberately shut it, and returned to his place.

"Now then," said Adhemar sharply, "now that we are private, be so good as to explain why you have abandoned this place to servants and are living abroad. I suppose you have done something of which you are ashamed and cannot face living here where all our fathers lived."

The color rose under Sigmund's dark skin. "Who the devil are you to—"

"Be quiet. I also hear that you have some idea of turning this place into a hotel—this place! Have you no sense of decency at all, no idea of your duty to your family, your property, your house, and your people? You propose to emigrate to America, I hear. In my day, emigration was the last resort of persons no longer fit to remain at home. Sigmund, how dare you behave like this?"

"Silence!" roared Sigmund. "I shall call up the grooms and have you kicked out. I know all about you. Because you've inherited a face like the Graf Adhemar's you think you can palm yourself off as the rightful heir, you bastard!"

"I beg your pardon?"

"I said you were the Graf Adhemar's bastard—"

"Fool. I am the Graf Adhemar."

"That's your story. Because he went off with a barmaid—"

Adhemar moved suddenly and Sigmund stopped in midsentence.

"When I said I was the Graf Adhemar Hildebrand, I meant it. Look, Sigmund, look."

Sigmund stared angrily and saw the figure in the chair become very slowly less solid and more transparent. The armchair had a leather back with the von Grauhugel arms stamped upon it; quite gradually Sigmund became aware that he could see them plainly, the colored quarterings, the open-grilled helmet with its crest of an eagle bearing off a lamb, the ribbon below the shield with the one word *Tenacitas.* Sigmund's eyes dazzled and there was a loud singing noise in his ears.

A moment later he became aware that he was sitting in a chair by the open window, he was leaning forward, and there was a hand on the back of his neck, pressing heavily.

"That is better," said a voice which sounded unnaturally loud. "Put your head between your knees, you'll soon recover. Franz, the cognac, quick. Bring it here. Sigmund, drink this."

The voice became normal in tone and Sigmund sat up to sip cognac from a glass held to his lips by the man who had called himself Adhemar Hildebrand and done something odd—oh yes, vanished away. Sigmund rubbed his eyes.

"You look quite solid now," he said vaguely.

"I am when I choose to be. Do you realize now who I am or shall I do it again? It's quite easy. Or Franz can do it just as well."

"Thank you, no. Stupid of me to faint, never done such a thing before. I—it can't be true. You used to walk about the corridors at night, gray and indistinct, not solid like this. Why—I don't believe it. I'm not well, I've got a fever. I shall wake up in a minute and find this is all a dream. And a damned silly one."

"Wake up, then," said the Graf Adhemar, and shook him violently. "Wake up, you stupid boy. Stand up. Walk. Now sit down again. You are awake, you know. Don't gape at me like that, I shall lose my patience in a minute."

"But I can't be talking to the ghost of—"

There came the sound of a ringing slap and Sigmund sprang up with a hand to his face.

"Now do you believe it? Or would you like to challenge me to a duel?"

Sigmund scowled for a moment, then his mouth twitched and he broke into a laugh.

"Not if you can fight as you did when you were alive, if all the stories are true!"

"That's better. If you really want to know, I can. Get the Herr Whatmore to show you the duel sequence in that film of his. Well now, if we've got past that nonsense, kindly tell me why you are not living here, looking after the place and the people as a von Grauhugel should."

"Because I have always been afraid that you—that is, that the Graf Adhemar married the innkeeper's daughter. Because you took the Gräfin's Ring, you know."

"Quite right. I did marry her. What about it?"

"She disappeared. If she had had a son and he had had sons after him—"

"You would not have been Graf. No, of course not. You need not have been so anxious, the Gräfin Cecilie was drowned with me. What happened was this: we came down the Rhine by water because I wanted her to see it, she leaned against a rail insecurely fastened, and it gave way. She— I dived in after her and Franz after me. That's all. If you want details about the wedding, ask Whatmore. I told him all about it and he did not believe a single word."

Sigmund drew a long breath.

"If I had known—I was always haunted by the idea that someday someone would turn up with the Gräfin's Ring and a whole set of proofs to show who he was, and I should be nothing and nobody and have to turn out from here and go away to make a living and a fresh name for myself somewhere else. It came to the point where I could not even bear to be here, in this house. So I thought I would go before I was pushed out and at least have a place in the world I'd made for myself. I couldn't be sure of anything—why the hell couldn't you speak before?"

"I also wanted something," said Adhemar.

"What?"

"I want my wife acknowledged. Entered in the family records, admitted to her right place. Taken up from her nameless grave at Wittlaer by Düsseldorf and buried beside me in Grauhugel churchyard with the ceremonies due to her rank. With a suitable inscription saying that she was

Cecilie, my wife—you can compose it, and if you do it clumsily I'll come back and haunt you in earnest this time."

"But of course—"

"At last, thank heaven, I have got a reasonably sensible descendant—collateral descendant—who is not so wilfully blinded by prejudice and wicked family pride as your father, your grandfather, his father, and, worst of the lot, my mother, Beatrix von Wittelsbach."

"But surely, if you had explained—"

"Sigmund. Do you really believe they would have listened? Acknowledged the despised Gutmann girl as one of the family?"

Sigmund thought of his father's remarks on the subject and agreed. "They were a narrow-minded lot," he said.

"Besides, I had not the power. They did not want me, so I could not speak. It was only the excellent Whatmore and his film that set everyone thinking and talking about me, so that the old affection came back, with good old Klaus in particular. Your idea actually, I believe. Thank you, Sigmund. Oh, one other thing before I go. Could you, do you think, pull down that quite hideous memorial of mine and replace it with something that didn't turn a poor ghost quite green every time he has to pass it?"

Sigmund laughed and said that he would see what could be done. "It is a horrible excrescence," he said.

"Oh, and cut some of my less probable virtues. Well, is that all?"

"Just a moment. Does anybody here know who and what you are and, if so, who?"

"Klaus suspects. The Herr Denmead guessed it almost from the start though he never said a word to anyone, I believe. A good fellow, Denmead, have you met him? No, well, you'll like him. He used to hang about to meet me at night; he made no sign but he used to smile to himself. Another who guessed quite soon, and I practically told her myself, was of course, the Fräulein Aurea Goldie. I thought she had a right to know."

"I intend to marry her, if she will have me."

"So she told me. We got on very well together and I approve your choice, my dear boy."

"Thank you very much indeed, I am glad that you do. By the way, it's quite fantastic your calling me 'my dear boy' when I'm ten years older than you."

"Nonsense, you're eighty years younger. Well, once more, is there anything else?"

"One thing more. The ring, may I have it?"

"You will find the Gräfin's Ring, Sigmund, where it ought to be, on the finger of the Gräfin Cecilie. They were honest folk who found her, they did not steal it. You will set it on the finger of the Gräfin Aurea, with my blessing. I have your word that you will do what I want done?"

"You have my word," said the Graf Sigmund steadily. "Though," he added in a lighter tone, "there may be trouble if I start knocking down your memorial. The village thinks it so beautiful."

The Graf Adhemar made a laughing gesture of despair.

"Now," he said, "let us drink a glass of wine together before we part, I also like your Malaga. Franz, the wine and two glasses."

"May I suggest three glasses?" said Sigmund. "I should like to drink with Franz also, if you will allow it."

"Certainly," said Adhemar. "Franz will be honored. Pour out a third, Franz. By the way, Sigmund, I regret that there is a dent in the backplate of Maximilian's armor in the upper hall. Franz fell down the great stairway in it."

"He was wearing it? I don't mind in the least," said Sigmund, "but what on earth for? I wouldn't put on that ton of metal for any money."

"I am given to understand that he was chasing a housemaid."

"Then she got away," said Sigmund crisply, and Franz set the filled glasses upon the table. "Didn't she?"

"Yes, Highborn."

"Well now," said Adhemar, picking up a glass. "Long life and happiness to you, Sigmund, with your charming Aurea. *Hoch!*"

"Thank you," murmured Sigmund, glass in hand, "but what can I wish you?"

"*Güte reisen?*" suggested Adhemar, "for after all these years I am going home."

"I remember when I was in Scotland," said Sigmund, "a toast to one going on a journey. How did it go? 'A soft path to the far traveller,' Herr Reisenfern."

Adhemar laughed and bowed. "Very appropriate. Thank you so much. Most kind."

Sigmund drank, set down his glass, and turned away to the window.

"I wish you were not going," he said impulsively. "Not so soon."

He heard two distinct taps behind him as two glasses were set down, but no one spoke, and after a moment he turned round. There were two empty glasses on the table with the last of the wine spiralling slowly into the bottom of each bowl, but otherwise the room was quite empty.

THE END

Rue Morgue Press Titles as of January 2001

Brief Candles by Manning Coles. From Topper to Aunt Dimity, mystery readers have embraced the cozy ghost story. Four of the best were written by Manning Coles, the creator of the witty Tommy Hambledon spy novels. First published in 1954, *Brief Candles* is likely to produce more laughs than chills as a young couple vacationing in France run into two gentlemen with decidedly old-world manners. What they don't know is that James and Charles Latimer are ancestors of theirs who shuffled off this mortal coil some 80 years earlier when, emboldened by strong drink and with only a pet monkey and an aged waiter as allies, the two made a valiant, foolish and quite fatal attempt to halt a German advance during the Franco-Prussian War of 1870. Now these two ectoplasmic gentlemen and their spectral pet monkey Ulysses have been summoned from their unmarked graves because their visiting relatives are in serious trouble. But before they can solve the younger Latimers' problems, the three benevolent spirits light brief candles of insanity for a tipsy policeman, a recalcitrant banker, a convocation of English ghostbusters, and a card-playing rogue who's wanted for murder. "As felicitously foolish as a collaboration of (P.G.) Wodehouse and Thorne Smith."—Anthony Boucher. "For those who like something out of the ordinary. Lighthearted, very funny.'—*The Sunday Times*. "A gay, most readable story."—*The Daily Telegraph*.   0-915230-24-0 $14.00

Happy Returns by Manning Coles. The ghostly Latimers and their pet spectral monkey Ulysses return from the grave when Uncle Quentin finds himself in need of their help—it seems the old boy is being pursued by an old flame who won't take no for an answer in her quest to get him to the altar. Along the way, our courteous and honest spooks, learn how to drive a car, thwart a couple of bank robbers, unleash a bevy of circus animals on an unsuspecting French town, help out the odd person or two and even "solve" a murder—with the help of the victim. The laughs start practically from the first page and don't stop until Ulysses slides down the bannister, glass of wine in hand, to drink a toast to returning old friends. "You'll never forget the secne when Ulysses frees a buch of circu animals who wreak havoic on a small French town. Thre's no sex, no gratuitous violence and not one four letter word but it's still as good as many current stories and fun way to spend an evening or two."—Manya Nogg, *I Love a Mystery*.   0-915230-31-3 $14.00

Come and Go by Manning Coles. This final book in the Latimer ghost trilogy finds our ectoplasmic heroes helping out a Bertie Wooster like nephew who is running away from aunt who would like to see him married and a couple of murderers who would like to see him dead. It started out simple enough. Young Richard Scorby didn't intend to make a fuss when the burglar broke into his apartment. After all, that's why he kept a very competent manservant about. But Wilkins was out of town an Richard was a little the worse for drink when he spotted the crook at his window. Instead of calling for a bobby, he reached for a perfectfully awful vase—a gift from his formidable Aunt Agatha—and with one well-aimed blow sent this second-story man hurling to the pavement. After which, Richard went to bed and was more than a bit perturbed when the police finally did show up to ask him if he knew anything about a burglar with a cracked skull. To Aunt Agatha, this was the last straw and she offered to find Richard a suitable wife. But before anyone could say "boo" Richard was off to Paris where he finds a trio of unlikely allies, two long-dead cousins and their fun-loving, if spectral, monkey.   0-95230-34-8 $14.00

The Chinese Chop by Juanita Sheridan. The postwar housing crunch finds Janice Cameron, newly arrived in New York City from Hawaii, without a place to live until she answers an ad for a roommate. It turns out the advertiser is an acquaintance from Hawaii, Lily Wu, whom critic Anthony Boucher (for whom Bouchercon, the World

Mystery Convention, is named) described as "the exquisitely blended product of Eastern and Western cultures" and the only female sleuth that he "was devotedly in love with," citing "that odd mixture of respect for her professional skills and delight in her personal charms." First published in 1949, this ground-breaking book was the first of four to feature Lily and be told by her Watson, Janice, a first-time novelist. No sooner do Lily and Janice move into a rooming house in Washington Square than a corpse is found in the basement. In Lily Wu, Sheridan created one of the most believable—and memorable—female sleuths of her day.   **0-915230-32-1**   **$14.00**

Death on Milestone Buttress by Glyn Carr. Abercrombie ("Filthy") Lewker was looking forward to a fortnight of climbing in Wales after a grueling season touring England with his Shakespearean company. Young Hilary Bourne thought the fresh air would be a pleasant change from her dreary job at the bank, as well as a chance to renew her acquaintance with a certain young scientist. Neither one expected this bucolic outing to turn deadly but when one of their party is killed in an apparent accident during what should have been an easy climb on the Milestone Buttress, Filthy and Hilary turn detective. Nearly every member of the climbing party had reason to hate the victim but each one also had an alibi for the time of the murder. Working as a team, Filthy and Hilary retrace the route of the fatal climb before returning to their lodgings where, in the grand tradition of Nero Wolfe, Filthy confronts the suspects and points his finger at the only person who could have committed the crime. Filled with climbing details sure to appeal to both expert climbers and armchair mountaineers alike, *Death on Milestone Buttress* was published in England in 1951, the first of fifteen detective novels in which Abercrombie Lewker outwitted murderers on peaks scattered around the globe, from Wales to Switzerland to the Himalayas. "You'll get a taste of the Welsh countryside, will encounter names replete with consonants, will be exposed to numerous snippets from Shakespeare and will find Carr's novel a worthy representative of the cozies of two generations ago."–John A. Broussard, *I Love a Mystery*.   **0-915230-29-1**   **$14.00**

Black Corridors by Constance & Gwenyth Little. Some people go to the beach for their vacations, others go to the mountains. Jessie Warren's Aunt Isabel preferred checking herself intothe hospital where she thoroughly enjoyed a spot of bad health although the doctors were at a loss to spot any cause. As usual, Jessie and her sister tossed to see who would accompany Aunt Isabel to the hospital—and, as usual, Jessie lost. Jessie's mother pointed out that pampering her rich aunt might do her some good in the future, even if it means that Jessie has to miss a date or two with some promising beaux. Aunt Isabel insists on staying in her favorite room, which means the current patient has to be dispossessed. And when that man's black wallet turns up missing, just about everyone joins in the hunt. That's about the time someone decided to start killing blondes. For the first time in her life Jessie's glad to have her bright red hair, even if a certain doctor—who doesn't have the money or the looks of her other beaux—enjoys making fun of those flaming locks. But after Jessie stumbles across a couple of bodies and starts snooping around, the murderer figures the time has come to switch from blondes to redheads. First published in 1940, *Black Corridors* is Constance & Gwenyth Little at their wackiest best.   **0-915230-33-X**   **$14.00**

The Black Stocking by Constance & Gwenyth Little. Irene Hastings, who can't decide which of her two fiancés she should marry, is looking forward to a nice vacation, and everything would have been just fine had not her mousy friend Ann asked to be dropped off at an insane asylum so she could visit her sister. When the sister escapes, just about everyone, including a handsome young doctor, mistakes Irene for the runaway loony, and she is put up at an isolated private hospital under house arrest, pending final identification. Only there's not a bed to be had in the hospital. One of the staff is already sleeping in a tent on the grounds, so it's decided that Irene is to share a bedroom with young Dr. Ross Munster, much to the consternation of both parties. On the other hand, Irene's much-married mother Elise, an Auntie Mame type who rushes to her rescue, figures that the young doctor has son-in-law written all over him. She also figures there's plenty of room in that bedroom for herself as well. In the meantime, Irene runs into a headless nurse, a corpse that won't stay put, an empty coffin, a missing will, and a mysterious black stocking. As Elise would say, "Mong Dew!" First published in 1946. "Wacky....witty....madcap....highly recommended."—D.L. Browne, *I Love a Mystery.*   **0-915230-30-5 $14.00**

The Black-Headed Pins by Constance & Gwenyth Little. "...a zany, fun-loving puzzler spun by the sisters Little—it's celluloid screwball comedy printed on paper. The charm of this book lies in the lively banter between characters and the breakneck pace of the story."—Diane Plumley, *Dastardly Deeds.* "For a strong example of their work, try (this) very funny and inventive 1938 novel of a dysfunctional family Christmas." Jon L. Breen, *Ellery Queen's Mystery Magazine.*   **0-915230-25-9 $14.00**

The Black Gloves by Constance & Gwenyth Little. "I'm relishing every madcap moment."—*Murder Most Cozy.* Welcome to the Vickers estate near East Orange, New Jersey, where the middle class is destroying the neighborhood, erecting their horrid little cottages, playing on the Vickers tennis court, and generally disrupting the comfortable life of Hammond Vickers no end. Why does there also have to be a corpse in the cellar? First published in 1939.   **0-915230-20-8 $14.00**

The Black Honeymoon by Constance & Gwenyth Little. Can you murder someone with feathers? If you don't believe feathers are lethal, then you probably haven't read a Little mystery. No, Uncle Richard wasn't tickled to death—though we can't make the same guarantee for readers—but the hyper-allergic rich man did manage to sneeze himself into the hereafter. First published in 1944. Picked by Deadly Passions as onf the ten best presented mysteries of the year.   **0-915230-21-6 $14.00**

Great Black Kanba by Constance & Gwenyth Little. "If you love train mysteries as much as I do, hop on the Trans-Australia Railway in *Great Black Kanba*, a fast and funny 1944 novel by the talented (Littles)."—Jon L. Breen, *Ellery Queen's Mystery Magazine.* "I have decided to add *Kanba* to my favorite mysteries of all time list!...a zany ride I'll definitely take again and again."—Diane Plumley in the Murder Ink newsletter. When a young American woman wakes up on an Australian train with a bump on her head and no memory, she suddenly finds out that she's engaged to two different men and the chief suspect in a murder case. It all adds up to some delightful mischief—call it Cornell Woolrich on laughing gas.   **0-915230-22-4 $14.00**

The Grey Mist Murders by Constance & Gwenyth Little. Who—or what—is the mysterious figure that emerges from the grey mist to strike down several passengers on the final leg of a round-the-world sea voyage? Is it the same shadowy entity that persists in leaving three matches outside Lady Marsh's cabin every morning? And why does one flimsy negligee seem to pop up at every turn? When Carla Bray first heard things go bump in the night, she hardly expected to find a corpse in the adjoining cabin. Nor did she expect to find herself the chief suspect in the murders. This 1938 effort was the Littles' first book.   **0-915230-26-7 $14.00**

The Black Paw by Constance & Gwenyth Little. From the 1941 dustjacket copy: Callie Drake, charming, bat-brained, and trouble attracting, undertook to assist a friend and was immediately involved in a first-class mess. Callie had intended to some highly justifiable petty larceny, but the police figured that murder was the motive for her appearance in the Barton household masquerading as a housemaid. It was true that Callie was the last person to have seen George, whose religious visions kept him up late at night, and it was Callie's room in which Frannie Barton met her death. Callie saw the isolated print of an animal's paw, and Callie saw the rocking chair swaying when no one was in the room. **0-915230-37-2** **$14.00**

Murder is a Collector's Item by Elizabeth Dean. "(It) froths over with the same effervescent humor as the best Hepburn-Grant films."—Sujata Massey. "Completely enjoyable."—*New York Times.* "Fast and funny."—*The New Yorker.* Twenty-six-year-old Emma Marsh isn't much at spelling or geography and perhaps she butchers the odd literary quotation or two, but she's a keen judge of character and more than able to hold her own when it comes to selling antiques or solving murders. Originally published in 1939, *Murder is a Collector's Item* was the first of three books featuring Emma. Smoothly written and sparkling with dry, sophisticated humor, this milestone combines an intriguing puzzle with an entertaining portrait of a self-possessed young woman on her own at the end of the Great Depression. **0-915230-19-4** **$14.00**

Murder is a Serious Business by Elizabeth Dean. It's 1940 and the Thirsty Thirties are over but you couldn't tell it by the gang at J. Graham Antiques, where clerk Emma Marsh, her would-be criminologist boyfriend Hank, and boss Jeff Graham trade barbs in between shots of scotch when they aren't bothered by the rare customer. Trouble starts when Emma and crew head for a weekend at Amos Currier's country estate to inventory the man's antiques collection. It isn't long before the bodies start falling and once again Emma is forced to turn sleuth in order to prove that her boss isn't a killer. "Judging from (this book) it's too bad she didn't write a few more."—Mary Ann Steel, *I Love a Mystery.* **0-915230-28-3** **$14.95**

Murder, Chop Chop by James Norman. "The book has the butter-wouldn't-melt-in-his-mouth cool of Rick in *Casablanca*."—*The Rocky Mountain News.* "Amuses the reader no end."—*Mystery News.* "This long out-of-print masterpiece is intricately plotted, full of eccentric characters and very humorous indeed. Highly recommended."—*Mysteries by Mail.* Meet Gimiendo Hernandez Quinto, a gigantic Mexican who once rode with Pancho Villa and who now trains *guerrilleros* for the Nationalist Chinese government when he isn't solving murders. At his side is a beautiful Eurasian known as Mountain of Virtue, a woman as dangerous to men as she is irresistible. Together they look into the murder of Abe Harrow, an ambulance driver who appears to have died at three different times. There's also a cipher or two to crack, a train with a mind of its own, and Chiang Kai-shek's false teeth, which have gone mysteriously missing. First published in 1942. **0-915230-16-X** **$13.00**

Death at The Dog by Joanna Cannan. "Worthy of being discussed in the same breath with an Agatha Christie or Josephine Tey...anyone who enjoys Golden Age mysteries will surely enjoy this one."—Sally Fellows, *Mystery News.* "Skilled writing and brilliant characterization."—*Times of London.* "An excellent English rural tale."—Jacques Barzun & Wendell Hertig Taylor in *A Catalogue of Crime.* Set in late 1939 during the first anxious months of World War II, *Death at The Dog*, which was first published in 1941, is a wonderful example of the classic English detective novel that first flourished between the two World Wars. Set in a picturesque village filled with thatched-roof-cottages, eccentric villagers and genial pubs, it's as well-plotted as a Christie, with clues abundantly and fairly planted, and as deftly written as the best of the books by either Sayers or Marsh, filled with quotable lines and perceptive observations on the human condition. **0-915230-23-2** **$14.00**

They Rang Up the Police by Joanna Cannan. "Just delightful."—*Sleuth of Baker Street* Pick-of-the-Month. "A brilliantly plotted mystery...splendid character study...don't miss this one, folks. It's a keeper."—Sally Fellows, *Mystery News.* When Delia Cathcart and Major Willoughby disappear from their quiet English village one Saturday morning in July 1937, it looks like a simple case of a frustrated spinster running off for a bit of fun with a straying husband. But as the hours turn into days,

Inspector Guy Northeast begins to suspect that she may have been the victim of foul play. Never published in the United States, *They Rang Up the Police* appeared in England in 1939. **0-915230-27-5 $14.00**

Common or Garden Crime by Sheila Pim. Lucy Bex preferred Jane Austen or Trollop to the detective stories her brother Linnaeus gulped down but when a neighbor is murdered with monkshood harvested from Lucy's own garden, she's the one who turns detective and spots the crucial clue that prevents the wrong person from going to the gallows. Set in 1943 in the small town of Clonmeen on the outskirts of Dublin, this delightful tale was written by an author who was called "the Irish Angela Thirkell." The war in Europe seems very distant in neutral Ireland, though Lucy's nephew, an officer in the British army, is home on leave. Most of the residents are far more interested in how their gardens grow than what's happening on the Eastern Front or in Africa. Her detective novels were greeted with great critical acclaim from contemporary reviewers: "Do some more, Miss Pim."—*Sphere.* "Humour and shrewd observation of small town Irish life."—*Times Literary Supplement.* "Excellent characterization, considerable humour."—*Sphere.* "Wit and gaiety, ease and charm...the kind of story I long to thrust into people's hands."—*Illustrated London News.* "Vivacious as a wall lizard."—*Observer." A* truthful, humorous, and affectional picture of life in an Irish country town."—*Daily Herald.* "Thank you, Miss Pim."—*Evening Herald.* Today's critics were just as kind: "Her style has simplicity and easily conveys the atmosphere of her birthplace."—Jacques Barzun and Wendell Hertig Taylor, *A Catalogue of Crime.* **0-915230-36-4 $14.00**

Cook Up a Crime by Charlotte Murray Russell. "Perhaps the mother of today's 'cozy' mystery . . . amateur sleuth Jane has a personality guaranteed to entertain the most demanding reader."—Andy Plonka, *The Mystery Reader.* "Some wonderful old time recipes...highly recommended."—*Mysteries by Mail.* Meet Jane Amanda Edwards, a self-styled "full-fashioned" spinster who complains she hasn't looked at herself in a full-length mirror since Helen Hokinson started drawing for *The New Yorker.* But you can always count on Jane to look into other people's affairs, especially when there's a juicy murder case to investigate. In this 1951 title Jane goes searching for recipes (included between chapters) for a cookbook project and finds a body instead. And once again her lily-of-the-field brother Arthur goes looking for love, finds strong drink, and is eventually discovered clutching the murder weapon.   **0-915230-18-6 $13.00**

The Man from Tibet by Clyde B. Clason. Locked inside the Tibetan Room of his Chicago luxury apartment, the rich antiquarian was overheard repeating a forbidden occult chant under the watchful eyes of Buddhist gods. When the doors were opened it appeared that he had succumbed to a heart attack. But the elderly Roman historian and sometime amateur sleuth Theocritus Lucius Westborough is convinced that Adam Merriweather's death was anything but natural and that the weapon was an eighth century Tibetan manuscript. If it's murder, who could have done it, and how? Suspects abound. There's Tsongpun Bonbo, the gentle Tibetan lama from whom the manuscript was originally stolen; Chang, Merriweather's scholarly Tibetan secretary who had fled a Himalayan monastery; Merriweather's son Vincent, who disliked his father and stood to inherit a fortune; Dr. Jed Merriweather, the dead man's brother, who came to Chicago to beg for funds to continue his archaeological digs in Asia; Dr. Walters, the dead man's physician, who guarded a secret; and Janice Shelton, his young ward, who found herself being pushed by Merriweather into marrying his son. How the murder was accomplished has earned praise from such impossible crime connoisseurs as Robert C.S. Adey, who cited Clason's "highly original and practical locked-room murder method."   **0-915230-17-8 $14.00**

The Mirror by Marlys Millhiser. "Completely enjoyable."—*Library Journal.* "A great deal of fun."—*Publishers Weekly.* How could you not be intrigued, as one reviewer pointed out, by a novel in which "you find the main character marrying her own grand-father and giving birth to her own mother?" Such is the situation in Marlys Millhiser's classic novel (a Mystery Guild selection originally published by Putnam in 1978) of two women who end up living each other's lives after they look into an antique Chinese mirror. Twenty-year-old Shay Garrett is not aware that she's pregnant and is having second thoughts about marrying Marek Weir when she's suddenly transported back 78 years in time into the body of Brandy McCabe, her own grandmother, who is unwillingly about to be married off to miner Corbin Strock. Shay's in shock but she still recognizes that the picture of her grandfather that hangs in the family home doesn't resemble her husband-to-be. But marry Corbin she does and off she goes to the high mining town of Nederland, where this thoroughly modern young woman has to learn to cope with such things as wood cooking stoves and—to her—old-fashioned attitudes about sex. In the meantime, Brandy McCabe is finding it even harder to cope with life in the Boulder, Co., of 1978.   **0-915230-15-1**   **$14.95**

About The Rue Morgue Press

The Rue Morgue Press vintage mystery line is designed to bring back into print those books that were favorites of readers between the turn of the century and the 1960s. The editors welcome suggestions for reprints. To receive our catalog or make suggestions, write The Rue Morgue Press, P.O. Box 4119, Boulder, Colorado 80306. (1-800-699-6214).